NURSE AT VILLIERS

Nurse At Villiers

by

Elizabeth Kellier

Dales Large Print Books
Long Preston, North Yorkshire,
BD23 4ND, England.

British Library Cataloguing in Publication Data.

Kellier, Elizabeth
   Nurse at Villiers.

      A catalogue record of this book is
      available from the British Library

      ISBN   1-84262-360-5 pbk

First published in Great Britain in 1980 by Robert Hale Ltd.

Cover illustration © John Hancock by arrangement with
P.W.A. International Ltd.

The moral right of the author has been asserted

Published in Large Print 2005 by arrangement with
Robert Hale Ltd.

Dales Large Print is an imprint of Library Magna Books Ltd.

Printed and bound in Great Britain by
T.J. (International) Ltd., Cornwall, PL28 8RW

NURSE AT VILLIERS

Beautiful but wild, the Pyrenees loom above the château where Nurse Judith Seton struggles to cope with her difficult patient, Madame Ruddler, Villiers' land manager Garth Massingham, an odd assortment of other characters including her own happy-go-lucky cousin who arrives out of the blue, and the reckless Paul Guis. Then, discovering to her horror that someone is attempting to blackmail Madame Ruddler, Judith begins to suspect almost everyone. Events build up until, abruptly, Judith has to face the fact that here at Villiers she herself is in the greatest danger.

ONE

The journey from London had taken three hours and when the long white ambulance reached the docks at Dover it was still raining. Turning from her patient, Judith Seton threw an anxious glance at the grey expanse of sea outside. The waiting cross-channel ferry was already bobbing up and down like a top. Even that seemed an unfortunate omen.

'I'm cold,' Madame Ruddler complained. Her beringed hands, plump and large like the rest of her, tugged irritably at her fur coat. 'The sooner we leave this climate the better. I have not been really warm since arriving for my operation three weeks ago.'

'I'm sorry, Madame. It is quite late in the year though.'

'But, Nurse, on the Continent early October is as good as spring. Here, it is like mid-winter.'

Judith did not answer. She had learnt already that it was usually wiser not to argue. Her patient gestured towards the nearest window.

'I daresay it's possible to see through that dark glass? Then cast an eye about for our escort, please. He should have arrived on the quay by this time.'

'Yes, there is a man heading in our direction,' Judith said. He was dark, rather tall, heavy shouldered. And, as the ambulance slid to a stop on the wet tarmac and the driver and his companion came round to open the doors at the back, the newcomer reached them.

'I'm glad you're punctual, Massingham,' was Madame's greeting.

'One does one's best for an employer.' The English voice, unhurried, was deliberately sardonic. 'Anyway, how are you? I take it that the gall-bladder operation was a complete success?'

'Thank you, yes; though it cost enough. Still, private fees in France might have been even more and at least these London surgeons are excellent at their jobs.'

The other raised his eyebrows but, standing aside while the ambulance men unfolded a collapsible wheelchair, said nothing. Then Judith, collecting her patient's belongings together, was suddenly conscious of his gaze moving to herself. Glancing up, she met grey deep-set eyes with a look in them too intense for comfort.

'This is the nurse I've engaged for the next few weeks from St. Vincent's.' Madame, too, must have noticed his interest. Her hand waved in Judith's direction. 'She'll bring some of my things and perhaps you'll attend to the rest? I'll carry my jewel-case myself... You've booked me a first-class cabin for the crossing, I hope?'

'Yes, all is arranged and after we've been through customs you can be taken on board at once. I've a steward standing by to show us the way.'

Following the retinue through the customs shed, then pressing through the crowds near the gangway, Judith felt conspicuous in her uniform. The ambulance men had said goodbye and left now. Two burly porters had taken their place. And more than a few of the other passengers, seeing Madame cocooned in her furs and blankets like some enormous chrysalis, stared curiously at the slim girl behind her in her navy and red cape.

Avoiding their gaze, Judith glanced surreptitiously at the man striding along just a step or two away from her. Then, unexpectedly, he suddenly fell back.

'Perhaps we'd better introduce ourselves properly. Madame is apt to ignore some of the social niceties when it comes to her staff. My name's Garth Massingham.'

'Mine is Seton, Judith Seton.' She had to look up at him, he was three or four inches taller than herself. 'May I ask what kind of job you have with Madame?'

'I'm the manager of her late husband's estate.'

'The place we're heading for – Villiers?'

'That's right. I've been there about twenty months, ever since Monsieur Ruddler died in fact.'

'Is it a big place?'

He nodded. 'Yes, there's quite a lot of land plus a couple of outlying farms. The nearest town is Lourdes and the Spanish border isn't very far away. Ever been in those parts?'

Judith shook her head.

'Ah well, you'll like the country thereabouts – if perhaps nothing else...'

Judith's open and attractive face registered momentary surprise. His words had been cynical, seeming to make an extra shadow on the choppy seas pointing towards the shore of France. And she wanted to ask exactly what he meant, what lay in front of her so that she could be prepared. But there was something about his attitude, the line of masculine profile, that was suddenly remote. So it was easier just to say: 'Have you travelled across especially to accompany Madame back like this?'

Again he gave that cursory nod. He was, she supposed, in his early thirties. 'I flew to Paris last night and came here by boat this morning – although I couldn't see the necessity for it myself.' He spoke with the impatience of a man dragged from what he considered important work to a minor and therefore irksome task.

'Perhaps Madame feels safer journeying across the Continent in the company of a man?' Judith felt obliged to point out.

'More likely she feels those jewels of hers are,' was the retort. 'However, as you've doubtless discovered for yourself by now, once our esteemed employer gets an over-sized bee in her bonnet reasoned argument is pointless. She must have led you quite a dance in the hospital?'

'No.' The brown of Judith's eyes held their own question. Why did such a man choose to work for someone he clearly did not much like? 'Actually, I didn't nurse Madame myself in St. Vincent's. I was working in the surgical wards; Madame, of course, was in the private block.'

'Then how did you come to take on this chore of bringing her out to France?'

She hesitated. The memory of what had happened nearly two months ago was again like a searing pain in her chest. 'My brother's a doctor at the same hospital – houseman to the Consultant who operated on Madame.'

'So he told you about her case and arranged matters?'

'Yes.' It had been a way of escape... For a few agonising seconds, she forgot the ship and the people around them and time was reversed. She was back in Roger's quarters, the letter containing the devastating news of her broken engagement still fluttering in her hand. It was all off, she remembered how her voice had trembled. John had met someone else.

For a moment, her brother – like herself – had been unable to assimilate the full import of the words. At the end of that month, her training finished, she had been due to go home in the Cotswolds and prepare for the wedding. 'But who is this other girl?' Still staring, he had led her to a chair. 'John can hardly know her.'

'Apparently he knows her well enough to want to marry her.' For the first time in her life bitterness had overwhelmed her. It had left the sting of acid in her throat. 'Remember he was going on a week's refresher course at his old agricultural college? This girl had just joined the clerical staff. It seems it was love at first sight. He said it was like being struck by lightning and even though they felt it was wrong there was nothing they could do about it.'

Behind their spectacles Roger's gentle eyes had acquired a sceptical look. 'Sounds extremely melodramatic and more like infatuation. You can hope it is, you know?'

'No.' The useless years, like the bitterness, she had tried to push back. 'No, it's better to face reality, to have the one clean break. But oh, Roger ... what am I going to do with myself? I can stay on here for a little while, but after that I'd like to get away – right away – just to think.'

Roger, a tower of strength in any crisis, had been a wonderful help. Then, just a few days ago, he had tentatively mentioned Madame Ruddler.

'If you're still set on the idea of going abroad – there's a patient in the private block who needs a trained nurse to accompany her to her home in the Pyrenees. She's English but her late husband was French.'

'What's been wrong with her?' Judith had asked.

'She's had a cholecystectomy, the gall bladder removed. There's also a history of cardiac trouble over twenty months ago, though her heart's not too bad at present. It's a matter of leading a sensible life and taking things easy.'

'She's fit enough to travel all that way?'

Roger had shrugged. 'We're not in favour of her going yet, she could have done with a long convalescence. But she's adamant and the only thing she'll abide by is our stipulation that she engages a nurse to look after her for a couple of months.'

Consequently, Judith had been introduced to Madame Ruddler that same evening, determined to take the post in spite of Roger's warning that she wouldn't have too compliant a patient to deal with.

Reaching their allocated cabin on the ferry

and attempting to make her charge comfortable for the three-hour crossing, Judith reflected ironically on her brother's habit of understatement.

'Good heavens, Nurse, kindly don't lump my pillows up like that.' Madame frowned then indicated Garth Massingham who was bringing in the last of her luggage. 'Ask Mr. Massingham to help me sit forward while you try again.'

They struggled together and afterwards Madame sank back. 'That's better. Now hand me my jewel-case again, please. Yes, leave it by my side – under the blanket here. Then ring for a steward and order me a whisky.'

'But Madame, is that wise? Surely a cup of tea...'

The remonstrance was interrupted by a theatrical sigh. 'Oh, if you are going to quibble, Nurse, let someone else get it.' Her gaze flickered again towards her manager.

Leaning against the door, he half-shrugged. 'I'll fetch you a whole bottle if that's what you want. I'll go to the bar.'

'Mr. Massingham?' It took Judith but a second to make up her mind and hurry out after him. He turned and, waiting for her to reach him in the corridor, allowed his gaze to move coolly over her slender-waisted figure. Suspecting he was purposely setting out to discomfort her, she raised her chin.

'You realise, of course, that I don't wish Madame to have this drink?'

'And you feel I'm helping to flout your authority, is that it?'

'Well, aren't you?' She was annoyed by his flash of indolent amusement. Two spots of angry colour surged into her cheeks. His eyes traced their outline, and in such a way as to give her the disturbing sensation that he had actually touched her flesh. 'After all...' she tried to make her voice cold, 'what happens to my patient is my responsibility. And allowing her whisky at this stage would in my opinion be most unwise.'

'All right.' She could see he was still amused. 'Be prepared for fireworks though.'

'I can't help that.' Her determination was feigned. Inwardly, thinking of that temper, she quailed slightly. 'The doctors didn't approve of Madame travelling this distance at all just yet – especially as she refused to fly.'

'She doesn't care for flying. At least one can't blame her for that.'

'No, but it would have made the journey easier. However, she would insist on coming.'

'Naturally,' His voice slipped into the kind of iciness for which she herself had striven a moment before. 'Even a call from the Archangel Michael wouldn't be strong enough to prevent our redoubtable employer from being at Villiers this next week.'

Puzzled, observing the change, the tightness, of his expression, Judith stared up into his face. But now his eyes were unfathomable and he was turning away. 'Better get back to her,' was his advice. 'But don't say I didn't warn you about the trouble ahead.'

It was curious, she knew he was referring only to Madame's likely tantrum about the drink. Yet, as they parted and the engines in the bowels of the boat burst into sudden life, it seemed to her that his words moved too. Into another sphere. And there, in that place, they took on a darker significance.

TWO

By the time the ferry docked in Calais Judith had recognised the fact that the next few weeks would probably bring many a battle of wills with her patient. She had been engaged merely because it was expedient, it had been a means of placating those 'insistent doctors'. And, if she surrendered to the role without a struggle, she would be allocated the status of an extra maid, just another pair of hands to fetch and carry.

Once they had transferred to the boat train to Paris and Madame had been settled again in her first-class compartment, she escaped for a while into the corridor. The rain covering England had stopped over the Channel. Here, the flat countryside was still unwashed. Nostalgically, she imagined her parents' farm nestling in its lush green valley – and then, only too easily, went on to think of John.

'Nice and dependable...' her mother's daily, with a penchant for delivering little homilies, had once remarked. 'This swift, heady romance is all right for some, but us Cotswold folk prefers to take things steady.' And Judith's mother, seemingly quite satisfied with her only daughter's prospects, had smilingly nodded.

Well, John – bowled over by a week's fleeting acquaintance with a girl from another part of the country altogether – had surprised them all. 'None of us can believe it,' her mother had written. 'Ever since you went round together as teenagers we've automatically linked your lives. It's incredible to know it's all over.'

Yes, over. The pain which had grown so familiar these past interminable weeks could still make her catch her breath. Wincing a little, at the same time thrown off balance by a lurch of the train on the tracks, she turned and stumbled against a hard, masculine chest. 'Oh, I'm sorry...'

It was Garth Massingham. She hadn't noticed him appear at the other end of the carriage and walk towards her. So far during the journey she had seen practically nothing of him. At each stage he had hung around just long enough to carry out whatever he considered his duties, the supervision of porters and such like, then had strode off nonchalantly in the direction of what Judith presumed was the bar and other male company. She supposed he was, in his way, as difficult a person to cope with as Madame herself.

Aware that his arm had gone out to support her, she straightened quickly. 'Thank you.' Her voice was formal.

He stepped back. 'How's our employer?'

She grimaced. 'Still non-too-pleased, I'm afraid, at being deprived of her alcoholic drinks.'

'Pity you can't administer a hefty sedative.'

'Once we board the Pyrenean Express this evening she can have a couple of sleeping tablets for the overnight journey. What time is the train due to leave Paris?'

'About eleven, but from the Austerlitz – which means we've to change stations. I've made the required arrangements. There'll be a small ambulance car waiting at the Gare du Nord.'

The were passing through a small provincial town; reverberating against the buildings the sound of the train grew louder and Judith had to raise her voice, 'Will there be time for me to make a phone call before the express leaves, I wonder?'

Garth Massingham nodded. 'Plenty.'

'It might take a little while, I want to ring home.'

'You'll find that rather expensive,' was the laconic comment.

'My mother has suggested I reverse the charges.'

'Well, ask for the English-speaking section of the Continental Exchange and they'll put you through all right.'

'I hope so.' There was a glimmer of a smile. 'My mother has a phobia about boats and she'll be relieved to hear I'm back on terra firma.'

Garth Massingham was regarding her reflectively. 'You have a large family?'

'My parents and two brothers. The youngest, the doctor, I've already mentioned. The other shares the running of our farm with my father.' She felt at liberty to return the question. 'What about you?'

'My father lives in Scotland with his second wife. My mother died when I was a child – in my opinion largely as a result of her troubles in escaping from occupied France during the second world war.' His tone was brusque.

'I'm sorry. Was she French herself?'

'Yes. My father was a Suffolk man, they met and married in nineteen-forty-five.' He

19

turned away, concluding the subject. It had touched the raw sensitivity of some inner wound, that much was obvious.

Wondering but unable to help, Judith watched the blur of another ancient town fly past the window. Then, preparing to leave, she paused again. 'Mr. Massingham – there is one thing that concerns me about Madame: her jewel-case. Are its contents very valuable?'

'Judging by the way she clings to it it might contain the Imperial State Crown – or some dark secret of her past. Perhaps that's it?'

She ignored the sarcasm. 'But isn't she taking a risk? Carrying it about like this?'

'Maybe; but even at Villiers she often hawks it around with her. So I shouldn't let it worry you.'

It was mid-evening when they reached Paris. Glimpsing the Eiffel Tower, pavement cafés in their haze of coloured lights, Judith was moved by that sudden thrill which stabs at every visitor. The Arc de Triomphe, the Notre Dame, the Louvre ... famous names beckoned. But their journey across the city to the other station down streets she had never heard of at least avoided the rush of traffic.

The Pyrenean Express had just drawn into the platform. And having once more transferred Madame Ruddler, this time to a first-class couchette, the other two stepped back into the corridor for a breather. Then Garth paid off a couple of French porters and rejoined Judith.

'So the next stop for us is Lourdes – about eight tomorrow morning. We drive the odd twelve kilometres from there.'

'We'll have been travelling a long time,' Judith said.

'Yes, so I hope that you besides her ladyship will get some sleep tonight. There's no reason why you shouldn't. The couchettes are comfortable, with a good supply of blankets and pillows. Yours is next door, by the way; mine's the other side.' He glanced at his watch. 'Anyhow, the train won't be off for at least another half-hour, so you slip off and make your telephone call and I'll dance attendance on Madame.'

French had not been one of Judith's strong subjects at school but she managed to ask her way to a kiosk and to put the call through. It didn't take as long as she had expected. Her mother must have been waiting near the telephone.

'Are you all right, dear?' Mrs. Seton made no effort to disguise her anxiety. Judith pictured how she looked: a little like Roger, kind-eyed and now somewhat plump. They talked about the trip so far, in such a way on Mrs. Seton's part as to make it sound that her daughter had swum not sailed across the Channel.

21

'Yes, dear, but you've still a long distance to go,' was the answer to Judith's laughing reassurances. 'Aunt Mary and I were looking up your route this afternoon.'

'Oh yes?' Her mother's youngest sister was the one aunt Judith didn't much care for. She was critical and talkative, and apt to enjoy the occasional family crisis simply because of the opportunity it gave her for a bit of extra gossip. News of Judith's shattered engagement had taken her 'tut-tutting' to every relative and friend in the district.

'Actually, Aunt Mary asked if you'd be able to do her a favour...' Mrs. Seton spoke guardedly, aware that her sister had never been at the top of her children's popularity polls. 'It concerns Fenella.'

'What about her?' Fenella was Aunt Mary's nineteen-year old daughter. 'Didn't you write that she'd a job as a hotel receptionist in Spain?'

'That's right, San Sebastian. She's been there since early summer. But your Aunt's becoming rather worried.'

'But why?' Busy doing her nurse's training in London, Judith hadn't seen her cousin for almost a year.

'Because Fenella's always been a terrible correspondent, as you may remember, and your Aunt hasn't yet heard whether she intends to stay there for the winter or not. So, noticing on the map that you wouldn't be too far away from this Spanish resort, she wondered...'

'If I can contact Fenella and discover what her plans are, I suppose?' Judith suspected that her mother was making more of her cousin's negligence than was necessary just to deflect their conversation and thoughts away from her own reason for leaving the country. And, in the circumstances, she could only promise to assist in any way she could.

But as if there weren't enough difficult characters to contend with, she ruefully thought afterwards, Madame, Garth Massingham and heaven knew who else at Villiers – without having to bother about her somewhat flighty cousin too.

THREE

The train drew slowly into Lourdes next morning. Beyond, on the fringe of the town, was the river and on its outer bank lay the famous Catholic shrine. Shimmering in the early sun, the great three-tiered basilica rose up from a setting of trees, guarding the precincts of Bernadette's Grotto. The consecrated place, where over a century before the young peasant girl had received her many visions, could be seen very clearly. A mass was being said before the open altar, with a hundred flickering candles etched out against a backcloth of massive rocks.

The holiday season having run down, the number of ordinary pilgrims had diminished. But the sick were still being brought from all over the Continent and at the station one of the special medical trains from Italy had just drawn in. The platforms were awash with humanity: invalids of all ages, priests and nuns and – dealing with the stretchers with typical Latin volubility – a host of their voluntary helpers.

Here, Madame Ruddler in her borrowed wheelchair did not merit a second glance. Garth Massingham glanced about them. 'I'll go and see if Heinzmann's arrived with the car yet,' he said – then headed towards the station entrance.

Apart from a minor emergency arising from the temporary loss of Madame's jewel-case key, which she wore on a chain round her neck and which Judith had removed whilst helping her to wash, the overnight journey had been blessedly uneventful. Once the prescribed sleeping pill had been taken there had been, apart from an occasional snore, a surprising silence. Retiring to her own compartment, Judith had been the one to remain awake. It was the first time she had travelled overnight by train; and the noisy rumble, the quite alarming tilt on some of the bends, had prevented her from sleeping till the early hours. Then, at six o'clock, she had had to rouse Madame and assist her to dress again.

Garth Massingham had not put in an appearance till the last moment, just when Judith had been making a hopeful query about ordering breakfast.

'I'm afraid we must all wait till we reach Villiers, Nurse,' she had been told. 'I've spent enough on this journey as it is. That Insurance Company of mine and their tiresome clause about not travelling with my jewels unless under male protection has cost me quite a packet. When I get home I've a good mind to cancel their policy and change to a less discriminatory company.'

So Garth Massingham's comment about the jewels being the reason for his being ordered along had touched on the truth? Like Judith herself he had been used as a token gesture, to comply with the demands of another outside body, in this case the Insurance Company. Yet at no time had Madame entrusted him with the jewel case and on the one occasion when he had offered to make it his sole responsibility she had almost snatched it away. So who could blame him for his later indifference?

'Will you go and find out where that manager of mine has disappeared to, Nurse?'

Madame had quickly tired of waiting. 'I'd like to leave this depressing place.'

'Yes, of course.' Judith ascertained that the jewel-case was well-hidden beneath her patient's rug then hurried away. Coaches, taxies and buses stood about the station yard waiting for their passengers: pilgrims, tourists or the ordinary townspeople. But of Garth Massingham there was no sign. Glancing around, she exchanged a smile with an elderly woman on crutches and her companion, a handsome young cleric who so closely resembled the other he must have been her grandson. They were making towards a small fleet of ambulances on the right, and were part of the crowd from the Italian sick train. Madame had called the place depressing. Yet, seeing the faces about her, catching some of the animated conversation, Judith was struck by a quality she was to feel whenever she came to the town – everybody's joy at being here, no matter what their disabilities.

Caught in thought, she turned back – then was nearly knocked flying by a man stepping clumsily from the rear of a line of parked cars. Winded by the collision, which appeared to have had no effect whatsoever on the massive frame of the other, she stared down. 'My shoulder bag...'

It lay at her feet, open, her purse, passport and make-up scattered on the tarmac. The man grunted, growled something in what sounded like German, and watched her stoop to retrieve the contents. At first Judith thought he intended merely to walk away. But then, aware of wine-ridden breath near her face, she found he had bent beside her.

They straightened simultaneously. He was holding her powder-compact. And seeing his fingers grip it with such force it looked as if it were going to be squeezed out of shape, Judith promptly held out one hand.

'Thank you, M'sieur, merci.' For a moment it seemed as if she would have to ask him again. But then, with an odd slow shrug that made his huge shoulders rise and almost brush against the sides of his bullet-shaped head, he released his hold. Judith, anxious to end the awkward encounter, gave him a last strained smile.

'Heinzmann!...' Not knowing what else to do, she was returning to the station entrance when she heard Garth Massingham's voice. 'So you're here? I've been searching for you.' Then, as if the English had been a mistake there was a spate of German.

With a feeling of sudden apprehension, Judith had already stopped and looked round. The man being addressed was the one who had just bumped into her. So he was one of the people who made up Madame's staff? 'You'll like the country thereabouts, if nothing much else...' Garth

Massingham's previous remark now took on a more sinister ring. And, seated in the back of the car beside her employer a few minutes later, she had the unpleasant sensation of feeling Heinzmann's curious gaze seek her out in the driving mirror above his head.

Leaving the town, climbing the hill behind the basilica, they headed for open country. Now and again Garth Massingham turned from the front and briefly pointed out one or two sights to her, an ancient monastery, a château, a village clinging tenaciously to green slopes far above them. But apart from that and Madame's complaints about the often reckless manner of Heinzmann's driving, the journey continued in silence.

Slowly, the Pyrenees closed in on the large black car. Mountainous white peaks flattered the blue of a cloudless morning sky. A lonely air set in. And during the next few kilometres they met only one vehicle, an old farm lorry. Forced to pull to the side. Heinzmann snatched at the wheel, lurched his passengers and mumbled sourly in German.

Just as she had pondered on why Garth Massingham should work for someone he didn't like, Judith fell to wondering why Heinzmann, too, had sought employment away from his own country. Both men in their different ways left her puzzled, and the latter made her nervous as well. Would there be no-one at Villiers with whom she could strike up a friendly and sympathetic relationship?

They passed through the last sleepy village before their destination. The empty road beyond veered round in continual hairpin bends, pushing between woods that clung to the mountain sides. Finally, it dropped to a lower valley. And by a low crumbling wall they slowed, turned through rickety iron gate-posts, and drove up a long twisting drive.

The large grey house was set in a hollow. The front was dignified and plain. Once upon a time it would have made an effective even dramatic foil for ornamental gardens. But of these few signs remained. Now, presumably because Madame did not countenance the idea of employing more labour, only the lawns were tended. By Heinzmann, Judith later discovered, and in any event what flowers could have proliferated under the care of those enormous hands?

As the car skidded to a stop, throwing up bits of gravel, Villiers' front door slowly opened. Three people appeared, two women in aprons – maids presumably – one middle-aged, the other flamboyantly dark and young, and, coming to the fore and so revealing her superior role, a smart blonde woman dressed in navy.

'That's Marcelle Guis. Must be in her mid-thirties I suppose. She's a divorcée but uses her maiden name.' Garth Massingham, having helped to extricate Madame from the car and started her on the ponderous journey into the house, dropped back to Judith's side. The maids had taken the luggage and she was at the rear of the procession, carrying the rugs.

'Is she the housekeeper?' They spoke in a near whisper.

'Yes.' They watched her take a firmer grip of her mistress's arm. Welcoming her home, she had not acknowledged anyone else – though, for an instant, the shrewd blue eyes had flicked sharply in Judith's direction.

'Has she been here long?'

'About as long as I have. Before that, apparently, there was quite a succession of housekeepers. Madame's brother-in-law persuaded this one to come.'

She was quite well entrenched then? At the murmur of their voices Marcelle Guis glanced round half-disapprovingly. Garth, with typical masculine arrogance ignored her – which made Judith feel more uncomfortable. It was clear from her manner that Marcelle Guis was jealous of her authority here in the house. Would her position clash with her own while she was here? Judith wondered.

Seeking respite from a sudden gnawing foreboding, she paused before Villiers' waiting portals and looked back. To the east where the land rose again there were wooded slopes leading steeply upwards to red overhanging rocks; and far beyond those, towering in the sky, were some of the pinnacles of the encircling mountains. Winking and changing colour, they slowly turned from white to gold in the sun then merged with the underlying purple.

'It's quite a sight, isn't it?' Garth Massingham was still beside her. And she was surprised to see how his expression had altered. The tiny cynical lines round his mouth had been erased and his face was caught by a brooding gentleness.

Whatever he might think of the occupants of the house they were about to enter, one thing was transparently clear – he had an immense regard for the estate itself.

FOUR

Madame's bedroom, crammed with furniture and a vast double bed, resembled a setting for some historical farce. There were velvet curtains, intricately draped, and a huge coal fire hissed in the marble fireplace.

Nightclothes were spread ready on a chair, making it clear that Marcelle Guis expected her mistress to retire to bed. Noticing her

31

drawing back the counterpane, Judith tried to be tactful. 'It might be best for Madame to have a light breakfast before resting.' She smiled – but there was no answering expression on the other's smoothly-made-up face. Instead, turning to the younger maid who had followed them upstairs with cases, Marcelle Guis barked an order in French which Judith gathered was meant to set the girl back on her tasks in the kitchen. And the latter, unconcernedly, withdrew.

Meanwhile, panting – somewhat unnecessarily, Judith thought – since the two men had practically carried her upstairs – Madame Ruddler sat and fanned herself with one glove. So far, her only anxiety had been about her post. And when informed that nothing out of the ordinary had arrived she appeared to be relieved.

'Surely the mistress can do what she likes in her own home?' Marcelle Guis now remarked. 'This is not an hospital.'

Her English was good. She must have had plenty of practice. For, as Judith was quickly to realise, their employer – although often contemptuous of much that was British – idiosyncratically preferred her staff to use her native tongue.

'I don't dispute that.' Judith kept her voice pleasant. The other would make a formidable opponent, it was foolish to court trouble. 'But at the moment bed isn't necessary.'

'Most people would say she requires a week or two there. Madame has had an operation not a holiday in Cannes.' The sarcasm bounced. 'Also the journey was very long, *non?*'

'But she had a good sleep on the train.' Judith glanced quickly across the room, making sure that the subject of their discussion wasn't listening. 'The doctors want Madame to proceed carefully, but it would be wrong to treat her like a totally-incapacitated invalid, you know?'

'Very well.' The lips were pursed. 'But if Madame does have a set-back that, naturally, will be your responsibility.'

The animosity seemed to linger. And when the time came for Judith to be shown to her room the housekeeper sent the maid to do it. 'You do speak English, don't you?' Judith gave a self-deprecatory smile. 'I'm afraid my French is atrocious.'

The other nodded. 'I know a little.' She was older than Judith had first imagined. There was a voluptuous air of experience about her and, strolling across to the window, she left a trail of cheap scent. Judith, seeing that her case had been deposited on the bed, began to unpack it.

'What is your name?' she asked the other.
'Rosa.'
'That sounds Spanish.'
'My father, he came from over the border.

Now we live in the village with my married sister.'

'Then you aren't resident here at Villiers?' The mention of the border had reminded her of Fenella. Soon, she would write to her cousin, and if that brought no response she would telephone the hotel. 'What about the other employees?'

'Madame Drouet, she is like myself. She cycles in – how do you say? – daily.' Curious, the maid had glanced over her shoulder to scrutinize the clothes being lifted out of Judith's case. But her disappointed little moue indicated they weren't showy enough for her taste. Bored, deliberately wasting time, she turned back to the window.

'And Herr Heinzmann and Mr. Massingham?' Judith persisted. 'Surely they must live on the estate?'

'*Oui.* The first has a room in the old servants' quarters at the top of the house and Monsieur Massingham occupies what used to be a labourer's cottage. See, its chimney is visible through the trees here.'

Stowing her empty case on top of the wardrobe first, Judith joined her and followed the line of her pointing finger. The cottage's chimney pot needed repairing, that much was clear even from this distance. Her gaze dropped to the drive below. The car was just drawing away; presumably Heinzmann was about to garage it in one of the dilapidated buildings – probably once stables and coach-house – that she had previously glimpsed beyond the main house. Returning to her things, she slipped underwear and nightclothes into appropriate drawers. So that she could remain within earshot of her patient she had been given a room just along the corridor from Madame's.

'Rosa!' The irate call from Marcelle Guis came a few minutes later. The housekeeper entered without knocking. 'Why are you still up here? I sent you only to show Nurse the way.' Her eyes were angry. And because she spoke in English she made it plain that part of the blame was being apportioned to Judith.

'I'm sorry.' It was simpler to accept it all. 'I detained Rosa, I'm afraid, by asking her a little about herself.'

'Madame Ruddler and I do not permit the staff to gossip on duty. Besides, Villiers is a big place, there is no time to waste on chatter.' Frowning, the housekeeper watched Rosa stroll out – the maid indifferent, to the point of outright impertinence.

Then, seeing the housekeeper was about to follow, Judith spoke hurriedly. 'Oh, about my patient's breakfast, Madame Guis...'

The other was immediately on the defensive. 'There was nothing wrong with it, I hope? Madame has always adhered to the English custom of having bacon and eggs.'

'Perhaps.' Judith forced a smile. But Madame had been put on a low calorie diet now, she explained, it was imperative she should lose some weight and so reduce the strain on her heart. Accordingly, the hospital dietician had drawn up a detailed chart.

'Very well, I will study it before lunch,' the housekeeper agreed. 'But you'll have to bring it down to me.'

Villiers' kitchen had been modernized, but here and there traces of a more arduous domestic age remained. A long farmhouse table, scrubbed to a detergent whiteness over the years, contrasted oddly with plastic-topped sink units and a large modern cooker. In one corner was an old wooden bench. Sprawled across it was Heinzmann taking his morning refreshment – a large glass of what appeared to be hock. And Judith, talking about the diet sheet to Marcelle Guis, uneasily sensed his gaze upon them both.

He left before she did though, treading heavily across the red tiled floor in his muddy boots and disappearing without a word. The housekeeper glared at the marks he had left but did not comment. How did they get on together? Judith pondered. Since he seemed to be employed as general odd-job man in the house as well as about the garden and estate they must be forced to meet frequently. But no doubt the German, like Garth Massingham, practically ignored her censorious presence?

She had not seen Garth again. After Madame Ruddler had been taken to her room he had, with a nonchalant wave at Judith, shown his impatience to return to his own work and had left. She half-expected to meet him at lunch. But, waited on in a slapdash way by the older daily – Madame Drouet – she was compelled to dine by herself in the gloomy old dining-room.

Marcelle Guis, she later discovered, not deigning to eat with Rosa and the others, also took most of her meals alone. In addition to a bedroom on the main corridor of the first floor, the housekeeper had an office-cum-sitting-room in the domestic region.

The day passed slowly, but was – as Madame Ruddler had prophesied – like a spring one. However, at dusk the temperature dropped; and the house, Rosa and Madame Drouet having departed, became black and quiet. Judith served her patient with evening dinner, then with Madame's somewhat grudging permission went downstairs for her own meal.

'With the staff situation as it is,' Marcelle Guis had informed her earlier, 'I can't provide cooked meals twice a day – except, of course, for Madame. The rest of us must manage with a cold buffet in the evenings.'

It was laid out on a large antique sideboard in the dining-room. Judith helped herself to cold chicken and a rather oily salad then ate without enjoyment. No-one came in, though at one point she imagined there were voices coming from the distant kitchen. But when she took her dirty plates there shortly afterwards the place was empty. Intending to collect Madame Ruddler's tray, she walked back upstairs and turned down the dimly-lit corridor. She was almost upon the partly-open door before realising that there was a discussion going on behind it – and that it concerned herself.

'Trained nurses aren't cheap,' Madame was saying. 'She is costing me a lot.'

'But, my dear, your operation wound has healed now, *non?*' To Judith's surprise it was a man's voice. 'And the stitches have gone? So in another week or so why should you require a nurse at all?'

'Exactly, Madame.' This was Marcelle Guis. 'Can't I care for you equally well?'

'Perhaps.' Madame sounded rather tetchy. 'But, unfortunately, I am committed to paying Nurse's salary for at least another calendar month – so she has to stay. Still, if there is not enough for her to do for me eventually, she must make herself useful elsewhere in the house.'

'You think so, Madame?' Marcelle Guis

was sceptical. 'Nowadays nurses have their own ideas.'

'No, they will not willingly take on domestic chores.' The support came from the unknown man.

'Well, I can't be expected to pay her for doing nothing, Gerard,' Madame retorted.

'I must meet her, this M'selle,' he said in answer.

And that you shall do, Judith silently promised with sudden determination. And right this minute.

Her rap on the open door must have startled them all. Walking in, she saw them posed like a trio of wax figures, Madame Ruddler still on the bed where she had lain since afternoon and the others on either side. 'Good evening?' She looked directly at the newcomer.

'Bonsoir, M'selle...' His recovery was swift. Tall and thin, probably in his mid-forties, he wasn't good-looking, his face was too long and bony for that; yet such was his charm that one immediately seemed to forget his disadvantages. 'So you, following in your Florence Nightingale tradition, are the lady of the lamp? It is a pleasure to meet someone of your noble profession.' He was bowing over Judith's outstretched hand, holding it to his lips for a second, then smiling into her slightly surprised eyes. 'I am Gerard Ruddler, M'selle, the step-brother of Madame's late husband. We were born of the same father – I of his second marriage, which accounted for my being very much younger.'

'I see.' The other two remained silent, watching somewhat resentfully as Gerard Ruddler, noting Judith remove Madame's tray from the locker, afterwards insisted on taking it from her.

'But I have to go down to the kitchen in any event,' Judith protested. 'I've to make Madame an evening drink.'

'Than I shall escort you there *and* back,' the Frenchman smilingly persisted.

'Have you come far, M'sieur?' Judith asked, as they descended the main staircase together.

'From Monaco, M'selle.' His English was fluent and, like Marcelle Guis, he seemed resigned to his sister-in-law's refusal to speak the language of her adopted country unless absolutely necessary. 'I had financial business to discuss with an acquaintance there. Now, because of further business, I have to go on to Paris and my apartment for a night or two. Had the situation been otherwise I would have escorted Madame home from hospital myself – instead of M'sieur Massingham. It was I who accompanied her to London in the first place.'

'I didn't know that.'

'I would have stayed but her surgeon

assured me it was not essential.'

'You must have arrived here tonight while I was having my evening meal?' Judith then commented, recalling the voices she had heard.

'*Oui*, it is possible. My hired car took me round the side. I wished not to disturb the invalid by making a noise at the front. But when Madame Guis let me in she said it was all right to go on up. We used the back, the servants' stairs; from the rear of the house it makes the shortest route. You must remember that for the sake of you own feet, *non?*'

In the kitchen, while Judith searched for a milk saucepan, he helped by finding a cup and saucer – then said: 'What do the doctors think of Madame's health at present, M'selle?'

Realising that this could have been why he wanted to conduct her downstairs – to question her alone – Judith gave him the basic facts. 'So...' he spread his slim hands wide, 'the prognosis is fairly good? Madame may yet achieve her century?'

'Well, she might have a good few years before her if nothing happens to aggravate that old heart condition.'

Absent-mindedly brushing a speck of fluff from his sleeve, he thoughtfully absorbed the remark. In the brighter light of the kitchen she had already noticed just how immaculately he was dressed: the silk handkerchief in the top pocket of his expensive, well-cut suit could have been ironed in place. And the many hours of travelling had had no detrimental effect on his soft white shirt.

'M'selle Seton ... or may I dispense with the tiresome formalities and call you by your first name, at least in private? Thank you... Yes, that suits you – Judith has a strong ring, yet still sounds very feminine.' The little digression over, he stood close to her arm, speaking very earnestly. 'You will understand my anxiety better than anyone, I am sure? In this matter of my sister-in-law's welfare I am under an obligation to my dead step-brother. We have no other family, I myself have long been a widower – so it is my duty to attend to her well-being, you see?'

'Yes, I can guess how you feel.'

'I am glad. My concern for her is why I made this long detour tonight – and is why I shall come back for a while as soon as possible.'

No nurse with a genuine interest in their patient could have failed to respond to such solicitude on the part of a relative. And in him Judith perceived her first certain ally in this isolated house. He, of all people, would sympathise with her own desire to do her best for Madame – in spite of all the difficulties. The thought was strongly com-

42

forting, making her smile at him.

It was only then that she became aware that Marcelle Guis, too, had now come down to the kitchen – and was standing by the door viewing the two of them together with something akin to jealousy moving across her face.

FIVE

Judith's first night at Villiers was a restless one. Several times she slipped along to Madame Ruddler's room. But, as on the train, the sedative had done its work and her patient, a large uneven mound in the great bed, snored rhythmically on in the darkness. Ascertaining that the tiny brass handbell was still in a convenient place on the bedside table, she crept out.

One o'clock came – and she was startled to hear the heavy tread of a man passing her door: Heinzmann, defiantly using the main staircase instead of the servants', and presumably heading for his bed. She heard him stumble and swear, softly – but with the venom of a man who has had too much to drink.

Then she fell into a shallow, dream-filled sleep. And the house became a cavern, deep and frighteningly black – with its occupants flitting across her mind like ghosts then dropping, shrieking, into the cavern's yawning entrance.

Next morning, helping her patient to wash and dress after breakfast she still felt jaded. 'I'll wear that long black frock, Nurse,' Madame concluded. It was really too tight and in it Madame looked like a dowager duchess, but the decision had taken an age. 'Don't jerk the fastening together though. There now see what's happened – you've broken the chain round my neck.' The one she wore to hold the key to her jewel-case. Irritably, she pulled the key free and stuffed it into her handbag. 'Now I shall have to purchase another.'

'I'm sorry, Madame.' It was simpler to apologise than to point out that it had been the other's own impatient tugging that had done the damage.

'Get Mr. Massingham to arrange for Heinzmann to run you into Lourdes one day to pick one up for me.'

The prospect of travelling alone with the German produced in Judith an involuntary flutter of alarm. But Madame was going on:

'And speaking of my manager, I'd like you to take him a message. Kindly tell him the accountants are coming this afternoon, so we'll need his papers.'

Judith went to try and find him while her

patient was having coffee. Pleased to be out of the house again, she wandered first down the drive and was about half-way down when she caught the sound of an approaching vehicle. It was being driven very fast, and as the young man at the wheel of the open-topped sports car rounded the bend in front of her his braking was noisy and sharp.

'Good-morning,' Judith said, as he stopped dead beside her.

'Oh, you are English?' He pushed back his wind-tumbled hair. His eyes were very blue – reminding her of somebody else's, though she could not straightaway remember whose. 'Do not tell me you are the nurse who is to look after Madame Ruddler,' he was saying. Before coming out she had thrown a cotton mackintosh over her uniform dress; its shiny pinkness suited her and his looks revealed the act. 'But I always thought that if a nurse were any good she must be an old sabre-toothed dragon, with starch right through to her under-clothes?'

'I don't care for your image,' Judith laughed. She had already glanced at the case wedged on the seat beside him. 'Forgive me, but you haven't come to stay at Villiers?'

'*Oui*, that is my intention – if I am allowed. My name is Paul Guis.'

She realised then where she had seen those eyes before, his resemblance to

Marcelle Guis was quite strong.

'You've met the housekeeper here?' he went on, 'well, I'm her kid brother. She practically brought me up...'

Their first meeting was necessarily short and after he had driven on Judith – about to proceed with her search – suddenly realised that their encounter had been witnessed by two others: Garth Massingham himself and a stout grey-haired man – whom she saw to be a priest. They had appeared at the top of the slope to her right and were strolling in her direction.

'Visitors seem to be arriving in pairs,' was Garth's dry comment when they reached her. 'First Gerard Ruddler and now Guis. Trust the latter to turn up like the proverbial bad penny at this time of year. I expect his summer engagement has ended and he's looking for a spot of free board before his winter job begins.'

In view of the priest's presence Judith thought it politic to ignore the last remark. 'Did you know the accountants are due at the house, too?'

'I guessed they wouldn't be long. I'm getting the farm accounts into order for them.'

'That's why I've been on the look-out for you – Madame wants you to have the first lot ready for this afternoon.' She paused. 'I do hope my patient isn't going to become too involved with these business matters?'

He grinned. 'Don't worry. It will hardly do her any harm. Quite the reverse – checking her money at this time of year seems to act as her personal tonic.'

And even a call from Archangel Gabriel wouldn't keep her from it? Judith, recalling his remark on the boat, now understood that this must be the main reason why Madame had insisted on coming home – the annual accounts. Even her health was of secondary importance to her money, apparently.

'How is your charge progressing, Mademoiselle?' The Abbé Sauvan, having been introduced, regarded Judith with eyes which, probably because they had seen so much of the human condition, held a surfeit of compassion. But there was humour there, too, and as Judith afterwards asked about his own work it lent an added lustre to his smile.

'*Oui*, Mademoiselle, I live in the village, that is my parish. But, for my sins, I am also responsible for several outlying hamlets – so my little scattered flock of would-be miscreants manage to keep me on the move.'

'Do you ever call on Madame?'

'Occasionally, I try, not successfully I fear – she is an avowed agnostic.' He sighed. 'I have not been inside Villiers since her husband's sudden collapse and death twenty months ago. One of the maids, at the suggestion of the doctor, sent for me but the M'sieur had already passed from this world when I arrived.'

'Was he a Catholic?'

'A lapsed one.' The priest's gaze rested on Judith's face. A mountain breeze rustled the folds of his soutane. 'You are not of my church, I suppose, Mademoiselle?'

'No, I'm an Anglican.'

'Ah, yes, like my friend here. He took his father's faith.'

'For what it's worth at the moment.' Garth's smile was wry. 'My present attitude can hardly said to be Christian.'

Judith expected the Father to return the sally. Instead, he suddenly looked grave. 'My son...' she heard him murmur, 'do not become fanatical in your desire to right matters here.'

What did he mean by that? Judith felt that curiosity must lie like an open question-mark upon her face. But as the two men said goodbye neither seemed to have realised that the remark had made any impact on her.

'He seems a nice man,' was Judith's comment, as the Abbé's ancient car clattered off.

'Yes, he often calls on me as he passes.' They had begun to walk back and it was natural for Judith to talk about the estate. 'I must start finding my way about,' she remarked. 'It looks the sort of place one could take a walk in and quickly lose one's bearings.'

Garth was studying the sky. It was a habit that reminded her of her father, all the meteorological reports in the world wouldn't prevent him from reading the signs of the coming weather for himself. 'The wind's changing direction,' he observed, before passing to her comment. Then, one strong hand pointed. 'There's a track past the outbuildings on the far side of the house there. Keep to that and you'll eventually come out on that crop of distant rocks. It's quite a climb and there's a little wooden foot-bridge spanning a gully that needs taking with care – but once over and following the path round you'll come upon a beautiful view. The previous owner of Villiers, an amateur ornithologist, built a stone look-out post further up – but that would probably be too far for you. The other makes a splendid walk though.'

'When I've the opportunity I shall go,' she promised.

She felt Garth looking at her sideways then. 'If you can manage to escape for an hour this afternoon – whilst Madame is ensconced with her accountants – and would care for a drive around the farms – I'll be ready as soon as I've handed over my papers...'

'That would be lovely.' She tried to sound as casual as he had. But, under the thrust of an unexpectedly warm anticipation, she could not prevent her voice from quickening a little.

Wondering where she was supposed to eat her lunch that day, Judith came downstairs after taking up her patient's meal to find Rosa heading towards the dining-room bearing a tureen of soup. The maid gave a careless toss of her head. 'You are to come in here,' she said.

'I'm to dine with Monsieur Ruddler?'

'Yes, he asked for you – Madame Guis intended to send a tray to your room.' Rosa leered, not because she cared where Judith ate but it had pleased her to see her superior's arrangements baulked for once. 'The M'sieur is already at the table.'

He wasn't the only one. Paul Guis was there too. Both men rose as she entered. 'Ah, the fair rose of England.' Gerard Ruddler pulled out a chair for her.

Paul grinned. 'I told the M'sieur how we had met – and he kindly invited me to join you.'

Gerard Ruddler picked up a bottle of wine. 'I brought this with me – the vintage should suit almost any palate.' He opened and tasted it with the air of the natural connoisseur, offered a glass to Judith and when she refused poured out more for himself and Paul – who drank with relish.

Gerard, savouring the experience with rather more finesse, then turned to giving Judith his attention. He had the sort of unhurried, easy approach when concentrating on a person that could be extremely flattering – as Judith had observed during his frequent visits to her patient that morning. Really, it was astonishing how even a woman like Madame could blossom out in the presence of an agreeable and polished man.

'You have another car, *mon ami?*' As their meal continued he glanced again at Paul. 'The one standing outside is surely not that which you had when we met here before?'

'No. I bought this only recently – from an American. I still owe him quite a bit of money, but we have a special arrangement whereby I pay him month by month.'

'Do you own a car?' Judith asked the older Frenchman.

'I am afraid I do not even drive – hence the necessity of always having to hire. Do you?'

'Yes. My brother and' – she almost said 'my fiancé' but changed it in time – 'a friend taught me in turns last year.'

'Then you must have been made into something of an expert, having a couple of teachers,' Paul inserted with his mischievous grin. 'Perhaps you would care for a ride in my new machine. We shall make a date, *non?*'

The dining-room door had opened though. Rosa had been the one to bring in the other courses but the sweet was carried in by Marcelle Guis herself. And it was clear that she had heard Paul's invitation for her narrowed gaze spoke her disapproval.

'If anyone wants a second helping there is sufficient,' she said stiffly – and looking at the men.

'My dear Marcey, you are a godsend to a starving mortal.' Paul's smile, his use of the special pet-name forced his sister's expression to soften. In a way it reminded Judith of the change in Garth Massingham when he stood and regarded the estate. Human flesh remoulded by a wave of deep affection; in one case affection for a place and in the other for a person.

Not that it wasn't ironic, Judith thought – listening to Paul wax loquacious about himself as he took more advantage of the proffered wine. For had he been an outsider he might have roused in the older woman a very different reaction. Even to a person of the same generation his attitude to work seemed decidedly flippant. 'I believe you're one of the world's dilettanti,' Judith laughed at one point. 'Have you never had a steady job?' He had been so many things, croupier in Monte Carlo, ski instructor in Austria, professional guide in Rome...

He wagged one finger at her. 'But you funny girl. All of them have been steady – as you call it. Not one lasted less than four months and some a great deal more.'

'You're incorrigible.'

'Ah, I am not familiar with that term. Is it good or bad? Anyhow, can I help it if change is vital to me?'

Gerard Ruddler fastidiously wiped his mouth with his table napkin. 'You will settle down one day, my friend, when the right girl appears.'

They were leaving the dining-room when Paul caught Judith's arm and pulled her back. 'Do you mind if I ask – have you mentioned my arrival to Madame by any chance?'

'Madame Ruddler?' Out of the corner of her eye Judith saw Marcelle come into the hall and hover in the background, listening. 'No, I haven't.' Chatting to Madame in the usual friendly manner of nurses to their patients wasn't easy.

'So, since Gerard Ruddler did not himself realise I was here till we met at lunch, nobody else can have told her either?' Paul was smiling. 'Good. It is better for my sister to break the news, but she has to wait for the right moment.'

Madame had a scowl across her forehead almost as deep as the fold of her dewlap when Judith returned. 'You sometimes take an inordinate amount of time to eat a meal, Nurse,' she whined. 'I have been sitting here hoping to have my hair done.'

'I'm sorry.' Undoing the thick, mostly still-black hair from its chignon and using the silver brush from the dressing-table, Judith began what was to become a thrice-daily job.

'The entire staff seems to be doing what it likes,' Madame grumbled on. 'I have twice rung the bell to the kitchen. Where are the maids and Madame Guis?'

'I don't know about the first two – but Madame Guis is probably talking to her brother...'

'Not that Paul!' Judith's words had slipped out unintentionally and her hands were suddenly still. Madame shook her head free. 'What is *he* doing here? Ring that bell again, please, and keep your finger on it. I demand someone comes up and informs me what's going on in my own house.'

This time the call brought the house-keeper almost at once, and Madame Ruddler waved Judith away. 'Come back in a few minutes, Nurse.' Forgetting to put the brush down, Judith went towards the door; but the other was too impatient to wait. 'Madame Guis, I have just learnt that your young brother is here again?...' Judith heard her say to begin the altercation.

'Yes.' Marcelle Guis bit on her lip. 'But I

54

wasn't aware he was coming. He knew you were expected home with your nurse from hospital. It is only because he lost his *pied à terre* in Lyon and had nowhere else to go. His ski-instructor's job doesn't start again till after the snows.'

'But he surely cannot expect to remain here that long?'

'No, of course not. He'll have to get somewhere temporarily. But I do hope you'll allow him to stay a little while, Madame. He tells me he's been having headaches and I'm worried about his health. He needs building up.'

'He needs sleep, I daresay,' Madame grunted. 'He was always one for burning the candle at both ends like most young people today.'

'You may be right, Madame.' Marcelle Guis was forced to ingratiate herself. 'But I promise he won't disturb you in any way – and, naturally, I'll be responsible for his keep as usual...'

The sharp knock on Judith's door some minutes later was not unexpected. The hope that Marcelle Guis would return downstairs without seeking her out had already been discarded. Quailing slightly, Judith stood and waited.

There was an hardness already pressing down on the housekeeper's face and the emotion she had been forced to quell in her employer's presence new found outlet. 'So you did tell Madame about my brother? – in spite of his asking you not to meddle.'

'He didn't phrase it exactly like that,' Judith said drily. 'Anyway, I didn't do it deliberately, just without thinking. Though in any event the news of his arrival had to be broken at some point.'

'The time for doing so was up to me, not to someone out to make trouble.'

'Trouble? That's nonsense' But Judith stopped, the other's gaze had alighted on the bed-side table.

'What is that doing in here?'

'Madame's silver hair-brush? I carried it out with me by mistake.' The obvious implication in the question brought a wave of indignant colour to Judith's cheeks. 'I'm just about to take it back and finish doing my patient's hair.'

'Madame does not like her belongings to be moved without her permission. It seems to me that you ought to attend to doing your own duties properly before interfering in other people's matters. It would be much wiser...'

The last sentence held a definite threat. Afterwards it was easy to shrug and feign indifference but, as Judith well knew, things like that had a way of lying uppermost in the mind.

SIX

The trip round the farms with Garth that afternoon was taken in the estate's battered land-rover. All the vehicles and machinery belonging to Villiers were in the same poor condition, Judith was told by him. Even Madame's saloon wasn't serviced regularly.

'Nothing can be relied on,' he complained, and annoyance made his chin like a jutting rock. 'In order to keep mechanical things running properly one has to pay out some cash.'

'Perhaps Madame doesn't feel she has it to spare?'

'She has the money all right.' One brown hand jerked his frustration out on the gears. 'As far as one can gather her husband was one of those who emerged from the Second World War better off than before; and in addition he milked the estate and never ploughed back. That's why it's in such a run-down state. And Madame is no more interested in the care of the land than he was. She's no respect for it. It would be better if she'd sell to someone who has.'

'How did you hear about this job originally?' They were leaving the furthest of the farms, one beyond the village, when Judith ventured to put the question. She had sat beside him until then happily relaxed. A state she put down to the somewhat inordinate amount of wine she had consumed. At each place they had visited hospitable farmers, and their wives had pressed them into taking at least one glass.

'Father Sauvan got to hear of the vacancy,' Garth was replying, 'he mentioned it in one of his letters.'

'So you knew the Father before?'

'I met him when I came on a touring holiday about three years ago. We corresponded fairly regularly afterwards.' His sudden smile revealed his affection for the older man. 'We even conducted a game of chess by post once.'

'You play together now?'

'Every Thursday, at his place. He's quite an addict.' As they passed through the village, he pointed. 'That's his presbytery, the church is in the lane at the back. He'd probably be delighted to show you round if you'd like us to call?'

But she had to refuse, the time was getting on and her patient was due for another heart tablet very soon. Garth listened thoughtfully. 'I know Madame Ruddler had cardiac trouble just before I arrived here, but I was under the impression her heart wasn't too bad at present?'

'And providing she doesn't suffer any shock or undue strain it should stay that way. These tablets are just a safeguard, to ensure the blood-pressure remains steady.'

Coming to the last stretch before Villiers, Garth slowed to indicate a gap in the wall skirting the road, 'If you ever walk to the village that leads to a useful shortcut. Too risky to take in the dark, of course; but then, it's hardly likely you'll be around these parts at night.'

Judith laughed. 'No, the evenings will probably be the time when my patient keeps me hopping about the most.'

'The contrast between a hospital and private post must be great?' Garth remarked afterwards. 'Especially when one has plunged into a difficult household. Had much contact with Marcelle Guis yet?'

'Rather too much.' She told him about the scene after lunch.

'Ah, yes – when crossed she can become a veritable virago.'

'I'm surprised she kept her temper with Madame Ruddler.'

'She's too shrewd to jeopardise her job, it suits her for the present. She's in full charge and out here can save quite a lot towards the fashionable small restaurant she apparently hopes to have one day. Also, according to gossipy Rosa, she optimistically anticipates a nice little inheritance eventually.'

'From Madame Ruddler? Won't Gerard Ruddler be the main beneficiary though?'

'Perhaps. Not that the elegant Ruddler's any cause to be bothered by money. He was married to a wealthy Argentinian and when she passed away some ten years ago he naturally became a rich widower. So he'll hardly demur if Marcelle Guis figures a bit in his sister-in-law's will.'

'You mentioned yesterday that he actually brought her to Villiers?'

'Yes. Before that she'd been managing a little bistro on the Left Bank in Paris. I think Ruddler had known her for some time.'

'Was he responsible for bringing in Herr Heinzmann as well?'

'No, I did that hiring myself,' he said shortly. 'He came seeking a job and I decided to give him a chance.'

'I just wondered how he came to leave Germany?'

'He left some years ago – though he's never bothered to pick up much of the language here. Originally, he was planning to marry a French girl; but it seems she changed her mind.'

Because of his drinking habits? Judith wondered – remembering that stumbling gait of last night. But the top of the drive was coming into sight now and the outing was almost finished. The sudden wish that it wasn't came as a surprising little ache. But the countryside under its crystal-clear light, the presence of the man beside her and their companionable chatter were things she was reluctant to turn her back on. Yesterday and the day before, during their journey from English, Garth Massingham had seemed taciturn and hard to get along with. But today, in the open air and with the farming community he appeared to understand so well, he was almost like a different person.

'Thank you, that was a lovely afternoon – I did so enjoy it.' She hoped he would believe her.

Paul was the first person she saw on re-entering the house; in a desultory fashion he was looking through the afternoon post. Heinzmann usually fetched it from the village and Marcelle Guis sorted it out and left the letters in the hall.

'Hello?' Paul brightened at the sight of her. 'Been out?'

'Garth Massingham showed me something of the estate.'

His young handsome face showed a flickering interest. 'I never know what to make of that fellow coming to work in a lonely outback like this. To me he is something of a mystery.'

To me, too, Judith thought; but there was another thing on her mind. 'I'm sorry if I caused you embarrassment by disclosing to Madame prematurely that you were here,

Paul. I've no doubt your sister told you what happened? But it wasn't done intentionally.'

'I guessed that,' he said easily. 'And the matter was smoothed down all right in the end.'

She was mollified by his lack of rancour. Then, unfastening her coat, she said: 'Have the accountants gone?' She had ushered them in herself before leaving – a couple of characters who might have been escapees from a Dickens' novel, with black undertaker suits and the smell of musty ledgers about them.

'*Mais oui*; they finished their business for today about a quarter of an hour ago. Since then Madame has apparently kept herself busy by writing letters; she has just sent them down for Heinzmann to post.' His fingers tapped a couple of unstamped envelopes.

Judith noticed in passing that the one on top was addressed to an Insurance Company in London then, remembering the letter she had promised to write to her cousin, Fenella, felt the tug of conscience. 'San Sebastian isn't all that far away, is it?' she asked abruptly. 'Is it possible to reach it from here by bus or train?'

'San Sebastian? Why? Do you wish to go there?'

'Perhaps – if I can manage to wangle enough time off eventually. My cousin is working at the Hotel Granada there and I'd like to visit her.'

'Then let me take you.' He ignored her uncertainty. 'When you are ready, tell me – it is a firm arrangement.'

Afterwards, Judith wondered how long it would be before his disapproving sister came to know of their plan? And by the evening she had begun to regret even mentioning San Sebastian to him. There was no way of her knowing, of course, that Fate was already unravelling a string of other complications – and that such a journey was, in any event, to prove to be unnecessary.

SEVEN

After breakfast next morning, while Heinzmann was stumping in with coal for the bedroom fire, a task which he carried out with the utmost amount of noise twice a day, and Judith was making her patient's bed, news was brought by Marcelle Guis which caused Madame Ruddler's temper to deteriorate. The elder maid, Madame Drouet, had gone absent without notice.

'According to Rosa,' folding her hands, Marcelle Guis assumed a pose of deference at the end of the bed, 'she has gone north to see her sick father again.'

'Sick father! Every autumn we suffer this, the old man goes down with a touch of bronchitis and off Drouet rushes. You know why? She's afraid that one of these days he really will die and if she isn't there the rest of the family will get the pickings. The French are all the same.'

The housekeeper let the insult pass. 'You are probably right about her, Madame; it's a pity we can't get rid of her for good. But labour in the village is hard to come by.'

The other shrugged. But then, apparently reminded of the remarks she had made to her brother-in-law about Judith's salary, she suddenly threw in a crafty: 'Perhaps Nurse could provide a little help about the house though? – as we're in a fix.'

Judith was trapped. 'Well, I'll do what I can. At least I can keep this bedroom clean and my own,' she murmured. With a private grimace, she recalled her brother's admonition the morning they had left the hospital: 'Madame's a wily old bird, so don't let her turn you into a skivvy. You're going as a nurse, remember, to see her through her convalescence. Don't allow her to deprive you of your right to some off-duty every day either.'

Waiting for a couple more days, then realising she would have to make a stand for herself, Judith touched on that subject one morning before lunch. 'While you're taking a nap this afternoon, Madame, would you object if I slipped out for a walk?'

'Why do want to do that?' The reaction was prompt and somewhat suspicious.

'I need fresh air and some exercise,' Judith said firmly, continuing to dust the room. She was behindhand with her house-hold work that morning; Madame had taken an age over breakfast and had lain in bed till nearly eleven o'clock.

'You English and your crazy predilections!' It was often Madame's habit to overlook the fact that they shared the same nationality when it suited her – though she seemed to have no great feeling or loyalty towards any country. 'Well, go if you must.'

'I shan't be long away,' Judith reassured her. 'I'll be back in good time to prepare your afternoon tea.'

Taking the walk suggested by Garth, she headed for the outbuildings and picked up the path. Soon, having skirted a field and wood, she was out on the open hillside and following a steep twisting track. Years ago it must have been made and used by herds of goats. Now, parts were overgrown, covered with ferns and fading wild flowers; and here and there were stones that had fallen from the craggy flank of the mountainside much higher up. Then, still climbing, she came to the tiny bridge that Garth had described. Glad to be in sweater and trousers, she walked gingerly across then round the next bend of rocks. It was a view that hove up suddenly, and swung one to a stop.

A range of mountains stood in statuesque splendour against the orange sun: purple, green and white. It was the scene from Villiers enhanced a hundred times over.

She still had a sense of exhilaration on her return to the house. To her surprise Garth was in the hall – exchanging a word with Gerard Ruddler. Glad to see him, but choosing not to show it too openly, she smiled at both men. 'I've been taking the mountain walk Mr. Massingham here proposed,' she told the Frenchman.

His gaze moved over her face with a certain expertise. 'I do not need to ask if you have enjoyed it... Is it not wonderful, my friend,' he said to Garth, 'how the beauties of nature have the power to quicken not just the heart of the beholder but the looks also? The texture of M'selle's skin has become like silk. She shines with her pleasure.'

Perhaps the compliment was too flowery for Garth's taste, for his own remark to Judith dwelt severely on practicalities: 'You had no qualms about crossing the footbridge?'

'I had a second's queasiness,' she confessed. 'I didn't expect the gully to be so deep. If one slipped one could have a nasty accident up there.'

'Yes, it's sensible to stay away from the place immediately after rain.'

Judith turned back to Gerard Ruddler. 'Would you like some tea when I prepare Madame's, M'sieur?'

He expressed his appreciation – then added: 'By the way, I am going back to Paris this evening, by the overnight express. You remember I said I had to?'

'We shall miss you.' Her regret was genuine and he smiled his thanks.

'Madame Guis is packing for me even at this moment, so I must go up and give her a hand.'

'I thought the accountants had completed their work?' she said, left alone with Garth afterwards. She was referring to the papers in his hand.

'They have. These are time-sheets; I'm just going into the study to make up the men's weekly wage packets.' She had guessed that he would rarely enter the big house except on some such business. But then he surprised her. 'I've popped in two or three times this past couple of days – but you weren't around. I wondered how you were coping – and if you'd like another break? What about coming over to dinner one night?'

'At your cottage?'

An amused, half-sardonic grin caught at his mouth as he saw her sudden doubt. 'Yes

– not because it would provide a good opportunity for a big seduction scene. It's just because I can't see you being able to escape from attending to our esteemed employer long enough for me to take you into a suitable restaurant in town.'

She had flushed a little at his first words but attempted to play it down. 'But the cooking...'

'I can grill a decent chop or two – though I couldn't promise to please an Egon Ronay. Nor am I any great connoisseur of wine – like your debonair admirer there.'

'Admirer? You don't mean Gerard Ruddler?' Judith felt her flush become slightly deeper. 'I doubt I'm his type – and probably the reverse is true, too.'

He smiled but shrugged. 'There are two main kinds of Frenchmen, I suppose: the down-to-earth plain-speaking provincial or country-dweller, and the sophisticated smooth-tongued Parisian or suburbanite. The former's usually worth his weight in gold; but it's the latter who appeals to the female sex.'

'You make us women sound extremely gullible,' she said with a little heat. 'Anyway, you are half French. But I daresay there's no need to ask into which category you put yourself?'

His grin came back at that. 'Well, at least if you take up my invitation you won't drown in an excess of flattery. So let me know when you want to come...'

At nine that evening, Judith closed Madame's bedroom door behind her and paused to collect herself. 'Oh, there you are?' Paul was at the top of the stairs. He had been out in his car most of the day and they had not met since morning. 'Can you came down? I have a big surprise for you.'

'What kind of surprise?' Wearily, she pushed a strand of hair from her forehead. It was now over an hour since Gerard Ruddler's departure, and Madame – who obviously hadn't wanted him to go – had been behaving like a spoilt, thwarted child.

'Come and see,' Paul was insisting. 'It's in the drawing-room.'

'All right – but not straightaway. Madame wants an extra blanket putting on her bed first.' She headed towards the cupboard down the corridor where the linen and blankets were kept.

Ten minutes passed before she was free to comply with Paul's request. The house was quiet but, reaching the bottom of the stairs, she caught what sounded like a suppressed giggle. Puzzled, she opened the drawing-room door.

Sitting in one of the deep armchairs at the side of the ornate old fireplace was a fair-haired girl; Paul was perched on a stool by her feet. They had helped themselves to a drink from what Judith knew to be a bottle of Gerard Ruddler's whisky on the nearby table; yet, compared to something else, that fact was entirely inconsequential.

'Fenella!' Judith was staring at her cousin and the case at her side as if they had arrived from another planet.

'There! I was certain you would be astonished.' Paul, springing up and almost dropping his glass, had a smile right across his face.

'Darling Judith, how nice to see you.' Fenella untwined purple-trousered legs. 'Long time, no see.'

'Yes, about a year,' Judith said, as her cousin came across and pecked her cheek.

'Well you were entombed in that wretched hospital.'

And you, Judith thought, were flitting from job to job in Italy and Spain. 'But what are you doing here?' she asked, still in confusion.

'I'm in a bit of jam.' It didn't appear to worry her overmuch. Returning to her chair, Fenella waved a languid hand. 'Mum sent me your address in an airmail that arrived only this morning – that's why I headed in this direction when I departed.'

'I heard your mother was concerned about you, I intended to write you myself in a day or two. But what's happened to your job in San Sebastian?'

'I've left it. I didn't want to stay much longer in any case – now it's nearing the end of the season things were becoming dull. They were starting the cut-rate autumn and winter holidays and expecting hordes of old-age pensioners. Not my scene at all.' Fenella laughed, but at Paul.

'Oh, I do understand how you feel,' he said. 'I've just finished a summer occupation myself. In a casino. With few customers coming in, we were so bored we started playing the tables ourselves.'

The two of them laughed again. And Judith felt a burst of impatience. 'But why come to Villiers, Fenella? Especially at this time of night?'

'I didn't plan to be so late,' Fenella admitted, 'the journey took longer than anticipated. It was a case of hitchhiking, mostly in lorries. I finally reached Lourdes then took a taxi.'

From the ridiculous to the sublime, that was a typical example of Fenella's methods. Paul was still grinning. 'We both drove up at the same time; I'd noticed the lights of a car just behind me and wondered who was arriving. But as soon as Fenella got out and asked for you I guessed who she was.'

Judith's glance was suddenly sharp. 'Does your sister know she's here?'

'Not yet; she is upstairs in her room.'

As for anyone else, Gerard Ruddler had

71

gone and Heinzmann – who had driven him to the station, was still out.

'Do not be anxious.' Paul was very confident. 'This poor girl surely cannot be turned away at this hour? She must stay here tonight.'

'Stay here?' Judith's eyes were round.

'Why not? Madame Ruddler need not know. I shall go up and talk to Marcelle and arrange everything…'

After he had gone, Judith moved closer to her cousin. 'What happened in San Sebastian, to make you leave like this?'

Fenella took another sip of her drink. 'If you must know, darling, I had a row with the hotel manager.'

'What about?' Judith persisted.

'He was forever carping at me; and recently he'd raised some objections to my going out with a male guest. This morning everything came to a head. We both lost our tempers – and I departed. I had to leave lots of my things behind, in the care of the other receptionist. They'll have to be sent for later. Or collected.'

'But why didn't you make straight for home?'

'You know I can't stand the deadly peace of the Cotswolds for long. Christmas will be soon enough for that Besides, I didn't have sufficient cash and now I've spent what little I did have on that taxi fare.'

'You've saved nothing? Nor had any wages due?'

'The manager told me that as I wasn't giving him proper notice I wasn't entitled to a peseta.' Getting up, she flicked a half-smoked cigarette onto the hearth. Her beads and poncho swung provocatively. 'Actually, darling' – at least she was candid – 'I was hoping you might lend me something?'

So that was why she had made her way here? Judith might have guessed. 'I can probably manage a little. But what then?'

'Well, if I can stay overnight, tomorrow I'll try and hitch a ride on to Paris. I'll easily find another job there, the problem is having enough cash to see me through the first week.'

When Paul returned he was rubbing his hands. 'So that is fixed. We are to smuggle Fenella up to one of the bedrooms along the back corridor and you are to take her some sheets.'

'What did your sister say?' Judith's voice was edged with trepidation.

He laughed. 'It is better I do not tell you! A strange girl turning up to see *you* without Madame's permission, then staying in the place unbeknown to its owner... She would not be a party to such a conspiracy, she said. But I wheedled her round in the end...' His power to manipulate obviously pleased him. Fenella looked on admiringly.

73

Only Judith was unimpressed, realising that if anything went wrong Marcelle Guis would choose her as the scapegoat. Paul would not suffer. She bowed to a flurry of vexation against Fenella for pitching them into this awkward situation in the first place. 'Come along then – but quietly. If my employer ever finds out what we've done behind her back tonight there'll be terrible trouble.'

'I'll crawl like a snail if it suits you,' drawled her cousin – giggling a bit. 'And don't worry. I'm sure it will all turn out all right.'

She and Paul exchanged an odd glance of satisfaction as they parted. Judith saw it. But, fortunately for her peace of mind that night, misread its significance.

EIGHT

Fenella was still asleep when Judith slipped furtively into her room next morning. 'Oh, don't...' she moaned, as Judith drew the curtains and daylight tumbled in.

'I'm hoping to scrounge you some tea and rolls while getting my patient's breakfast. Come on, wake up.'

'Very well, don't bully me, darling. What I really need is a cigarette.' Stretching out a naked arm, Fenella reached for her bag.

Judith flopped down on the bed. It was almost ten o'clock. She had hoped to start Fenella on her way long before this, but her plans had gone disastrously awry. Madame had woken early for once, rung for attention, then instead of taking breakfast in bed had decided to go through the lengthy ritual of washing and dressing first.

'I've brought the money.' Judith put the envelope containing it on the table. 'There may be enough to take you part of the way by train.'

'Oh, thanks.' Fenella glanced at it then, lighting the cigarette, climbed out of bed and wandered across to the window. 'There's a couple of men in the grounds. Who are they?'

Judith joined her. 'Don't let them see you. They work here. The one's called Heinz-mann, the black-haired one is the English estate-manager – Garth Massingham.'

'Hmm; what with Paul you seem well supplied with the opposite sex. And that manager's quite a dish – the rugged type.'

Judith did not comment but turned towards the door. 'I'm hoping that Paul will give you a lift as far as the town. While you start dressing I'll go down to the kitchen.'

Rosa, leaning against the sink and preparing the vegetables for lunch, was the only one in there and to Judith's mention of

Madame Guis she said: 'I think she is still in her bedroom – she was arguing with her brother.'

'Arguing? What about?'

'I do not know. They were there when I went up to ask how many of these I had to do.' Rosa stabbed at the pile of potatoes in the bowl.

Smuggling up extra rolls and tea on the same tray as Madame's some time later, Judith chose to go by the back staircase. But it was a stratagem that didn't pay off, for at the bottom she met Marcelle Guis coming down. And she saw the other's eyes fill with a burst of impotent anger.

'I have just seen your cousin,' she was told. 'And for what is happening I blame you. You had no right to permit her to enter this house in the first instance.'

'I couldn't prevent her,' Judith answered. 'Anyway, what do you mean? – exactly what *is* happening?'

'You had better go up there and find out for yourself... But I assure you the outcome would have been very different if it hadn't been for my concern about my brother's health. He needs to remain here, he needs building up and a rest.'

Fenella was laboriously making up her face when Judith returned. Sprawled across a chair, and watching her, was Paul. 'So here you are?' Judith said to him, and to her cousin: 'Why haven't you packed?' Her nightdress was still in a heap on the floor.

'Don't worry.' Paul shifted his position. 'There is no hurry – she is not going after all.'

So this was what had upset Marcelle Guis? For a second incredulity kept Judith speechless. 'Not going?'

'No.' Paul's smile vaunted their achievement. 'We have done some quick arranging in your absence.'

'So it seems. But just how can Fenella stay?'

'Simple. *She* needs a job – and here we have one. Temporarily, she is taking Madame Drouet's position. It is a good idea I have had, is it not?'

'You're crazy – Madame Ruddler would never consent.'

'She has done, under subtle duress, of course – while you were downstairs. My sister went in and told that she'd just heard from me that an English girl had turned up in the village, seeking work ... and as she'd extra people to cater for and wanted to keep up her standards in the kitchen – especially with M'sieur Ruddler returning – she wondered if she might engage her?...' His smile was a little sly. 'I daresay it was the mention of her dear Gerard that did the trick. Madame would not want his stomach to be neglected.'

77

Fenella, putting on lipstick, pursed her mouth. 'Naturally, no mention will be made of our being cousins, Judith, with our different surnames that won't be necessary.'

So it was all settled? 'How did you talk your sister into doing it, Paul?...' But Judith didn't actually put the question – for Marcelle Guis herself had already supplied the answer. She had obviously struggled against her brother's proposition – but he, using mild threats and cajolery and doubtless hinting that if Fenella didn't stay he mightn't either, had quickly got his way.

And now they were all caught up in an act of deception together. 'I don't like it,' Judith protested to Fenella afterwards.

Her cousin pulled a face. 'Darling, don't be an old square – nobody's actually telling lies, just withholding information.'

'In any case, you'll make such a rotten maid – and having seen Marcelle Guis now you ought to realise that the job's going to be no picnic. She's efficient and expects others to be as well.'

'I'll cope.' Fenella was remarkably casual about it all, the sudden change of her previous plan.

Too casual? Judith recalled that knowing little look that had passed between her cousin and Paul last night. They had discussed the possibility of Fenella staying on at Villiers even before she herself had entered the room – abruptly, Judith was convinced of that. Fenella, never reticent, must have revealed immediately that she was jobless; perhaps had even laughed and said, 'I suppose there's no vacancy for me here?' And Paul's little scheme for this morning, for her to take the absent Madame Drouet's place, must have begun to be formulated then. No wonder Fenella had been so unconcerned about getting up and packing, she had known all along that she probably would not be leaving.

Yet, curiously enough and rather to her relief, Judith saw her cousin only rarely during the next few days. She and Paul still ate most of their meals in the dining-room but that was a privilege Madame Guis was determined should not be extended to Fenella. 'The kitchen is the proper place for domestic staff,' she said firmly – adding, perhaps to baulk further opposition: 'Besides, when the M'sieur returns, what would Madame say if she knew one of her maids were sitting at the same table?'

Gerard Ruddler, true to his word, was soon back at Villiers. 'Madame's certainly missed you,' Judith told him one afternoon, after meeting him in the hall. He was studying his batch of mail – there was usually something forwarded on from Paris for him – and she was on her way out. Several times now she had taken the same walk up the mountain track.

Another time the Frenchman would have made some reference to her appearance. Today, in addition to trousers and anorak, she had a pale blue scarf tied gypsy-fashion about her head. But although his gaze took it in, he seemed rather pensive. 'I only wish I could help my sister-in-law more, Judith,' he confided. 'I have offered to take over the running of the business side of the house, for example. But she will not hear of it. All she will say is that she does not wish to impose further on my kindness.'

'I can understand that,' Judith said. Probably Madame was afraid that by allowing him to do more she would risk seeing less of him. 'But she's coming along very well, you know? In fact later on today I intend to suggest it's high time she started moving about the rest of the house.'

Fenella was standing in the drive when Gerard Ruddler escorted Judith to the door a second later. She had, apparently, just run into Garth and seeing her cousin appear she waved at her to join them.

'That looked to be an intimate farewell from our employer's brother-in-law,' she remarked, after explaining she was waiting for Paul – who was driving her to the village to buy cigarettes. 'The finger-tip kiss and the military-style click-click of the heels...'

'Oh, that's just Gerard Ruddler's way,'

Judith interrupted quickly – but avoiding Garth's eyes.

'Nevertheless...' Fenella went babbling on, 'don't forget the saying about the danger of being caught on the rebound. A girl from a broken engagement is apt to respond to fancy mannerisms like those...'

The age-old maxim had made the flush of self-consciousness shoot into Judith's face. But she struggled to make her words light. Fenella hadn't purposely meant to embarrass her, she was sure of that; having heard the news previously from her equally garrulous little mother, Fenella – though refraining from being over-demonstrative and only mentioning it once or twice – had made it clear that she was of the same mind about John as Judith's brother, she thought he had gone quite mad.

'I take it that you don't like Gerard Ruddler, Fenella?'

'Not much. And he certainly wasn't very pleased to discover I'd been hired in his absence. I heard him ask Marcelle Guis why she hadn't mentioned me when he rang up from Paris.'

'What did she say?'

'That, what with trying to connect his call to the extension in Madame's bedroom, it had slipped her mind. Or so my rough translation went. After that their French became too fast for me.'

'I expect he was thinking of his sister-in-law paying out extra wages. It seems he has some idea of shouldering financial matters for her on the domestic side – and probably showing his worth by cutting down a few expenses. However, his offer wasn't taken up, so your job seems secure enough for now.'

'Well, that's something.' At the approach of Paul's car from the distant garage, Fenella prepared to leave – but then turned gaily. 'Oh, by the way, in case you're wondering,' she called, 'I've told Garth who I am. He seemed so eminently trustworthy!'

Judith, silent afterwards, felt herself waiting almost tensely for the comments she sensed were bound to come. But Garth, clearly made thoughtful, deliberately took his time.

'I wondered from the first why a girl like you should have come to this medical desert,' he said at last. 'Now I know.'

Her chin was up. 'My cousin shouldn't have mentioned anything about my broken engagement.'

'Why not? It's nothing to be ashamed of. To use a cliché, one must just pick up the pieces and start again. There's no point in running away because of a damaged heart – or pride – to here or anywhere else.'

'I didn't run away, and pride had nothing to do with my decision.' Her voice was defiant. But she could not outstare those cool eyes, they had pierced the kernel of truth with too much facility. Well, perhaps she had done some running – from the possible pain of bumping into John again and from the ordeal of facing people at home. But she didn't want to admit it right now. So, driven to make a stand for herself, she sent out a retaliatory dart: 'Anyhow, as for my coming here – you did, didn't you?'

'Ah, yes, but I had a sound objective reason.'

A desire to right matters? – whatever the Abbé Sauvan had meant by that phrase. She wished she had the nerve to speak it out loud, to question *him* in turn. But even as she braced herself, the chance had gone.

'Still,' he was saying, 'I suppose this explains, in part at least, your reluctance to come and have dinner. I've been waiting for you to contact me. But all in vain it seems now.'

She bridled a little at his touch of mockery. 'I've not taken up your invitation simply because of the lack of opportunity to get away in the evening as yet.'

'You're sure you're not still fleeing from the masculine sex? – at least of the younger variety...'

'Of course not.' She ignored the further reference to Gerard Ruddler.

'Then if you can't join me for a meal, why not make it drinks? What about this week-end?'

'Very well.' She took it like a kind of challenge. 'I'll slip out for half-an-hour on Saturday night while Madame's having her dinner; there's no reason why I shouldn't.'

Her gaze swept beyond him then – to the clanking old land-rover coming up the drive. Heinzmann was at the wheel. Clambering out then reaching back inside for a shot-gun and a couple of dead rabbits, he turned his brawny frame in their direction and acknowledged Garth. The small limp bodies were still dripping blood and some of it was caked on the German's massive hands. It was a sight that remained with Judith even amongst the pure and rugged grandeur of the mountain slopes.

NINE

The suggestion that her patient should start moving about the house was not made till the following day after all. Judith, who had been awaiting the best opportunity, was bunching up the pillows and helping Madame to settle for her afternoon nap.

'...downstairs first, then a few quiet strolls through the grounds,' she said. 'And before we know where we are you'll be planning little shopping expeditions to the town.'

84

There was a tiny affronted silence. 'Are you trying hospital tactics on me, Nurse? I don't want to go out of this place until *I* am ready, thank you! You'll be endeavouring to hustle me along on one of your daily treks next.'

'I don't go walking every day,' Judith said sweetly, deciding to let the other simmer down again. There would be other times. 'This afternoon, for instance, I shall use my spare hour in penning a letter home.'

'It's astonishing to learn that Fenella is now with you,' her mother had just written. *'Aunt Mary received an airmail from her only this morning… She gave few details, trust Fenella! But when you answer this perhaps you'll tell us more?'*

The whole truth? At least Fenella had kept her promise to write; Judith had exacted that from her the first morning. But how she had chosen to slant her news could only be imagined: *'Darling Mum, you'll never guess – I came here to visit Judith on my day off and ended by being offered a job! So everything's great…'*

There would have been no mention of the job being temporary nor of the devious methods used in obtaining it.

But, beyond hinting at the former to prevent anyone at home being taken wholly unawares when Fenella moved on again, Judith kept her comments about her cousin down to a minimum.

Anyway, what could she say? – except that Fenella was very well. Employment at Villiers hadn't had any effect on her buoyancy – nor even on her hands, which still looked as though they had never in their life tackled any washing-up. How, under the eye of a woman like Marcelle Guis, she managed to evade so much work Judith could not imagine. And the amount of time she succeeded in taking off was amazing. So many evenings her bedroom was empty, with the bed unmade and discarded clothes lying in a heap. Presumably, she and Paul were making the most of the situation and going out quite a lot together.

An hour passed. Then, having written to Roger as well, Judith put her pen and paper away and walked along the corridor to look in on Madame. Expecting to find her still dozing, she was surprised to hear Garth's voice and the sounds of fierce disagreement.

'I tell you I shall have to have the money,' he was saying.

'And I tell you it's quite impossible.' Madame was almost spluttering. Judith, by the partly-open door, stood amazed.

'I warn you...'

'Don't start threatening me, Mr. Massing-ham!'

'Is that what you call it? Believe me, Madame Ruddler, you've heard nothing yet

– I don't give up that easily and I'll be back...'

He flung open the door, stormed out – and bumped straight into Judith. 'Oh, I'm sorry.'

'I should think so!' She saw that his pupils were pinpoints of black and that the darkness seemed to have cascaded down the rest of his face. She saw – but felt no sympathetic reaction – she was too provoked herself.

'What were you doing, upsetting my patient like that?' she demanded. 'You barged in, woke her up – and all without permission.'

'I didn't barge in,' he said, 'I knocked; and she was awake. As for obtaining permission from you, I wasn't aware that was necessary. You ought to draw up a list of rules and nail it to the door.'

'I might do that,' she rapped back. In spite of their mutual anger they both were struggling to control their voices so that Madame could not hear. 'It just never occurred to me that anybody would march in there and create a scene.'

His hands, looking as if they yearned to shake her, made an exasperated gesture. 'In your own way you're as infuriating as your boss... If there was a scene, she caused it; all I wanted was a calm and rational talk, a discussion.'

'But you were arguing about money.'

'Yes, I need it. I can't carry on without

cash. There are repairs to be done to the buildings, our machinery is breaking up... Getting anything done always means a fight, she's so stubborn.'

'Maybe. But you can't do battle with my patient at present. You will have to wait.' Her expression remained inflexible, like his.

'So that things get even worse?' His anger was fired afresh. 'No. She is surely not so ill now that she can't face up to some of her obligations on the estate? What that woman needs is a shock to bring her to her senses, some straight speaking. And, whether you approve or not, I intend to get money out of her somehow. I've had to do it before – and I'll do it again.'

'I won't allow you to upset her at this stage...' But she was speaking to the empty air. He had gone, his footsteps staccato on the stairs, leaving her alone.

The memory of their controversy worried Judith continually that evening. Had she blundered in too quickly? Been too aggressive towards Garth? Yet she knew that, as a nurse, she had a duty to protect her patient – so why should she regret taking a stand?

Then there was the effect of the disagreement on Madame – that bothered her as well. And although her charge ate a fair-sized dinner, simpered at her brother-in-law when he called to say good-night – in short, behaved much as usual – Judith kept on watching her as if converting every sign of normality into an ominous symptom.

She was settling Madame down for the night when she said: 'You remember your Consultant in London gave you a letter to hand on to your local practitioner, Madame... Isn't it about time we passed it on?'

The other, making sure the heavy water-jug on her bedside table was close enough to reach, glanced round. 'I am recovering satisfactorily, aren't I, Nurse? So what need have I to see any doctor at present?'

'But your French G.P. would probably be most interested to learn how your operation went.'

'Perhaps. But that interest would cost me unnecessary money, Nurse,' was the sour response. 'The French give nothing without payment, you know? At least that is *my* experience over the years. Why do you think I go out of my way to employ mostly foreigners?'

'But you find mercenary people of every nationality,' Judith remonstrated.

'The French can be worse than most. For money some of them stop at nothing.' The hand that had begun to fiddle with the tie of her bed-jacket gave a little jerk and the force of the next words seemed allied with that movement: 'Absolutely nothing – believe me – even blackmail...'

'Blackmail?' Judith, about to bend and help to remove the jacket, paused and stared. 'You're not implying, Madame, that someone has tried such a thing on you!...' It was later that she was to remember her employer's anxiety about the post on their return to Villiers and that slithering relief when informed there had been nothing unexpected. 'But that's such an odious crime.'

'Odious it may be, Nurse. But, if successful, it is also extremely lucrative.'

'Why should it be successful though? Nowadays, the police in any civilised country go to any length to stop such a racket.'

'Oh, the police...' It was wearily sarcastic. 'They are apt to stir up more of the past and even more trouble than anybody else. Only a fool would call them in. Still...' the plump fingers beat a nervous tattoo on the sheet, 'It is over now. After all these months, that final payment, there will surely be nothing else...'

'But, Madame...' The revelation had shaken Judith. She had remained poised on the other side of the bed, her wide eyes dominating her pretty face. 'Surely one shouldn't allow a blackmailer to escape scot-free? Whatever one has done in the past one shouldn't so easily submit?'

'You make it sound simple, Nurse. And in this case it was not. There was something held against my late husband, something that was supposed to have happened during the German Occupation of France in the war. And when the dead are involved there is little defence...'

'Nevertheless, Madame, you should have sought help from somebody. Had you no inkling who the blackmailer was?'

'No, Nurse – except that it was someone who clearly had discovered a great deal about my husband; there was knowledge I hadn't even been sure of myself.'

'But where do you think this blackmailer came from?'

The older woman looked surprised even to be asked. 'Why, from this area, of course. At least, that is what I deduced from their demand notes – which gave instructions where the money was to be left. Collection addresses were used – usually at hole-and-corner little shops. Different ones each time.'

'The person came from *this* area?' Outside, amongst that towering scenery, the sweet heady air of the Pyrenees? From a blessed town like Lourdes or little Betharram? Perhaps even nearer than that? Judith felt an added tremor of shock. 'But, Madame, he – or she – is probably still in this vicinity? Still here?...'

'Perhaps so. Who can say?'

'And you didn't recognise the writing in the demand notes?'

'Naturally not. Besides, the handwriting

was so obviously heavily disguised. Each word was in scrawled block letters.'

There was a closing-over of Madame's expression beginning though. And seeing that Judith wanted to pursue the subject, she vigorously shook her head.

'No, it is over now, as I've said. So there's no point is discussing the matter further, Nurse.'

TEN

Judith stayed sleepless that night. It seemed such an incredible thing to have heard that, as the black hours passed, she could half-believe she had imagined it. The wilful Madame Ruddler – once translated into the victim of a blackmailer? It seemed impossible. And the blackmailer might be still around?

In the cool clear light of that dawning Friday morning, it was even harder for her to assimilate such facts. Especially as Madame herself behaved as if nothing unusual had passed between them. Autocratic, aloof to all her staff, after a visit from her brother-in-law she was also disposed to be energetic.

'Today, Nurse,' she announced before eleven, 'I have decided to take my coffee downstairs.' She spoke as if the idea were her own, that Judith had not been pressing it for days. 'So please make certain the electric fire is switched on in the sitting-room and then bring Heinzmann back to assist you.' Satisfied, she closed the lid of her jewel-box; since her visitor had gone she had been busying herself making a list of the contents.

At the door Judith turned. 'What if Herr Heinzmann is working elsewhere? I can easily help you down by myself.'

'And risk a fall? No, if you can't find him bring Rosa or that new girl.'

By chance, Fenella was the first person Judith saw. Supposed to be dusting the hall, she was lolling against a table, flicking through a French magazine. 'Heinzmann?' she said. 'No, he's not around here. Actually, Garth is searching the house for him, too. I think he's gone up to Heinzmann's room. As for Rosa, she's cycled off to one of the farms to collect more milk.'

'Then you'd better come and help. Madame Ruddler has at last agreed to make a trip downstairs.'

A reluctant grimace contorted her cousin's pert face. Since that first morning, when Marcelle Guis had grimly conducted Fenella into their employer's presence and introduced her as the girl she had engaged from the village, she and Madame had had no reason to meet. Yet, in the bedroom a few seconds later, they were sizing one another up with the suspicious animosity of longstanding enemies. 'It's the generation gap,' Fenella remarked to Judith afterwards.

'Don't push me, girl,' Madame cried. 'You'll send me hurtling down these stairs.'

'She must weigh a ton,' commented Fenella, following Judith into the kitchen – where she had gone to make the coffee afterwards. 'I thought you said she'd been on a diet?'

'She still is. And according to the bathroom scales she's lost nearly a quarter of a stone.'

'You'd never guess it,' Fenella said, with all the tactlessness of her mother. 'She looks exactly the same to me.

Settling herself on the wooden bench, she watched her cousin walk to and fro. Under her overall she still wore her casual clothes and looked nothing like a maid. It was a calculated effect, Judith judged, not 'doing your own thing' at all but just a means of needling Marcelle Guis.

'You've awful dark rings under your eyes, darling,' was her next remark. 'Haven't you slept well?'

'No. I've been rather worried,' Judith said. 'What about?'

Judith hesitated. The temptation to confide in someone else – particularly a member of one's own family – was suddenly quite strong.

'Well?...' Fenella urged – and disposed to linger if it meant delaying the next phase of housework. 'Has your patient been playing you up?'

'No, it's not that. It's something she said. She didn't intend to tell me – it just slipped out.'

'What?' Curiosity was beginning to seep into Fenella's doll-like eyes. But the cousinly sympathy that was still there drew Judith on.

'You won't tell anyone?'

'Of course not.' With a grin, Fenella mimicked their old childhood cry: 'Cross my heart and hope to die.'

Judith took the plunge. 'Madame Ruddler's been blackmailed.'

Fenella stopped fooling about and stared in the way Judith had stared last night. 'Blackmailed!... You're joking!'

'Unfortunately, I'm not.'

'But whatever has she done that could lend itself to blackmail?'

'As far as I can gather it was her late husband who was up to something illegal. During the war. She divulged a few things – and then clammed up.'

'How frustrating.' Fenella, disappointed, bit on her lip, but then brightened. 'Not to worry though – patients do tend to carry on confiding in their nurses, so it's almost certain you'll learn a good deal more before long. You'll have to keep on providing her with suitable openings.' There was a noisy little whistle. 'Anyhow, what a turn-up for the books... Blackmailed! Madame Ruddler!'

'Don't raise your voice too much,' Judith warned quickly, glancing hastily at the door and seeing it was open a crack. 'I don't want anyone else to know.'

'Naturally. And I shan't tell a soul. In any case' – it was a rueful afterthought – 'who here at Villiers would believe me?'

Judith had the coffee-tray ready to take out when Fenella, still loathe to return to her tasks, said casually: 'Incidentally, darling, if you want anything from the town I'm going in this afternoon – with Garth. He learnt I wanted to go and offered to collect me.'

'Oh yes?' A moment passed while Judith absorbed the news. It shouldn't have affected her too much, but strangely, inexplicably, it did. 'What will Paul think of that?'

'He doesn't yet know. But it'll probably be good for him – to think he's facing a little competition.' Fenella's look changed. 'But what about *you*, darling? Do you mind?'

'Why on earth should I?' Under Fenella's undisguised scrutiny it was difficult for Judith to assume a naive surprise – but she tried.

'Well, Paul once told me that you and Garth seemed to get on fine together and that he'd spent one afternoon driving you round the estate.'

'He did. But I doubt he'd do anything so rash again...' The addition rang with sharp cynicism – which she had to explain: 'We had a clash of opinions about my patient yesterday afternoon – and we quarrelled.'

'Oh, if that's the case,' Fenella said candidly, 'that's probably why he offered me this lift today. It's a typical man's way of trying to get his own back.'

At least Judith was saved from attempting to reply to that, for the telephone rang in the hall and Fenella, sighing, went to answer it. 'The call was for Paul,' she said, meeting Judith again a few minutes later. 'He's taking it in the study. It's the American from whom he bought his car – he says Paul owes him another payment.'

During the afternoon – and more than once – Judith couldn't help thinking of Garth and Fenella together. Innocent though the outing might be, it pricked against her consciousness like a small troublesome burr.

Surely she couldn't be experiencing the insidious pangs of silly jealousy? she thought. The hurt of the past hadn't dimmed entirely yet. So how could her heart be reacting to the vagaries of a possible new love?

Stoking up the bedroom fire after bringing

Madame's afternoon tea, she was caught in a reverie, and the dancing tongues of flame seemed to twist and turn and become like a score of tantalising question-marks.

'Nurse?' Her patient, speaking from the bed, was the one to break her absorption. Madame had stayed downstairs for over two hours – attended for a good deal of that time by her willing brother-in-law. Then she had had a late lunch in her room and taken her customary nap. Now, in the middle of drinking her tea, she paused as if remembering something.

'Our conversation of last night, Nurse...'

'Yes?' Dismissing everything else from her mind, Judith walked to the bed.

Madame fidgeted awkwardly with her cup. 'You realise I told you in a moment of weakness... And that I wouldn't want you to mention the matter to anyone else?'

'I understand, Madame.' Guiltily remembering Fenella, Judith spoke clumsily herself. 'You don't think it might have been wise to have informed the M'sieur, your brother-in-law, though? At the time, I mean? He might have helped.'

The suggestion was almost fierily rejected. 'Why should Gerard have been involved? What happened in the past, when he was but a child, is no concern of his. There being such an age difference between them, he and my husband never had much contact.

No, I had to keep him out of it – and I preferred to deal with the whole unpleasant business on my own.'

The subject was being closed again – this time apparently for ever. And is if to stress the finality Madame changed her tone and gestured imperiously with the empty cup. 'And now – will you please pass my jewel-box over, Nurse? You know I always like it kept within reach.'

Judith glanced about the room. 'Where did you leave it?' she asked, remembering that the other had been sorting through its contents earlier.

'It's on the dressing-table there – where it's been since morning. I should have taken it downstairs with me – only you and that girl seemed to rush me so much I quite forgot.' She put the cup aside and fumbled in her bag for the key.

Judith took the box across then returned to the fireplace. And Madame's little cry of outrage made her jump.

'Madame? Whatever is wrong?'

Her patient, sitting erect in the bed, was staring at the opened box, her mouth transfixed into a rounded 'Oh'. 'One of my diamond rings,' she finally managed to choke, 'it's gone!'

Judith, too, was staring. 'Gone?'

'Yes! The box was already unlocked and the ring is missing. If I hadn't previously re-arranged everything, so that I knew exactly where each piece of jewellery lay, I might not have noticed the loss for days. I have been robbed!..'

ELEVEN

Primarily, it was the effect on her patient rather than the missing ring that engaged Judith's attention and concern. Madame had turned a beetroot red and her fingers had wound themselves about the jewel-box like straining tentacles.

'Press the bell to the kitchen and order Madame Guis to muster the staff here,' she eventually panted. 'I must tell Gerard as well. Go on, please; don't waste any more time.'

Judith tried to calm her. 'Just let me have another look round.'

'What's the point? The ring was safe enough in the box this morning; it can't have jumped out.'

'No, but it might have fallen. And a small article like that could easily have rolled along the floor without your noticing.'

'I tell you it was there when I closed the lid, Nurse.'

Judith yielded. 'Very well, I'll call Madame

Guis and your brother-in-law. As far as I know though hardly anyone else is in at present.'

'Who was in the house this morning? Did any strangers, any tradesmen, call?'

'I'm not certain. But from time to time all the rest of us were about.' Paul, Fenella, even Garth... Why should his name drop so suddenly into the mind? And couple itself so readily with the memory of yesterday afternoon? – when she had found him storming out of their employer's room, and afterwards heard him declare: 'I intend to get money out of her somehow...'

'Is the ring very valuable, Madame?' The question was spontaneous.

'It's not worth so much as one or two of the others, but on the open market it would fetch a very good price.'

'And nothing else is missing? You're sure?'

'A hundred per cent sure. My other rings are here, so are my brooches and pearls etc.'

Judith was puzzled. If someone had stolen the ring, why hadn't they taken the more expensive items as well? A thief from outside probably would not have hesitated. But what about a person actually in the house? Had this particular ring been chosen in the hope that it might not immediately be missed?

Listening to her patient's indignant speech to Marcelle Guis a few minutes later, she reluctantly remembered another remark of Garth's: 'What that woman needs is a shock...' Well, Madame had certainly had that. With frantic hands she clutched her handkerchief and frequently patted her forehead.

'I can hardly believe this, Madame! The ring has definitely disappeared?' When the housekeeper had first entered the room, she had adopted her usual deferential position at the end of the bed. But, as the news sank in, she stared as Judith had stared. 'You were sitting in that armchair this morning – I saw you with the jewel box on your lap myself – couldn't the ring have slipped down the side?'

'Nurse has already looked.'

'But how could anyone have got the key to the box? You keep it with you.' The house-keeper paused to consider. 'Unless you accidentally left it unlocked yourself?'

'I suppose I must have done.'

Marcelle Guis was glancing at Judith. 'It's strange that you didn't notice that Madame was forgetting to take her box down with her this morning. You know she likes it with her.'

'I never gave it a thought,' Judith said shortly, 'not at the time.'

'But what about later, while Madame was taking her coffee? Did you not come back to the bedroom at all?'

'Yes, I slipped up once or twice – to make sure the fire was all right. But I didn't think about the jewel box; I had no reason to.' This was becoming almost like a cross-examination and Judith was suddenly wary.

Marcelle pointed across the room. 'You've looked behind the cushions of the chair and felt down the back?'

'I did that as soon as Madame told me the ring had gone.'

'You could not have – missed – it?' The pauses were deliberate, and the blue eyes strayed to the dressing-table then lingered meaningly on the silver brush which Judith had absent-mindedly taken to her own room. 'Small things are so easily – over-looked.'

Hot with resentment, Judith said: 'I can make yet another search, if Madame herself wishes it.'

The latter dabbed again at her lips. 'It seems useless but you can try. And perhaps you, Madame Guis, will go and check on any outside callers today then question the rest of the staff? If I am harbouring a thief in my house they will rue the day they entered...'

Gerard Ruddler was the next to hurry into the room. And when Judith followed him downstairs some minutes later he was hurriedly discussing the matter in the hall with Marcelle Guis, Fenella and Garth.

Since the front door was still open it was obvious that the last two must have just returned from town and had been called in.

'This is a distressing business, Judith.' At her approach, Gerard Ruddler turned.

'What's going to be done?' said Fenella.

'I'm not yet sure,' Judith replied.

'Are the police going to be brought in?'

They were all waiting for the answer. And almost involuntarily Judith glanced at Garth's face, seeking for any sign of special apprehension in him.

'In due course probably. Apparently Madame prefers to take up one of your suggestions, M'sieur...' Her gaze shifted to Gerard Ruddler. 'She thinks it a good idea to try the services of a private investigator first.'

'Then she's made up her mind? I only tried that advice because I know how she hates ever becoming embroiled in ordinary officialdom.'

He was right. After he had gone, Madame had mused to Judith: 'Gerard's notion is a good one. And I've certainly little desire to have those busy-bodies of policemen marching into my place. Very likely, they'd soon be meddling in other affairs...' Had that been a worried reference to the business over which she had been blackmailed? The musing had tended to develop into a vituperation: 'Yes, I'll do it – there'll be time enough to call in the interfering law when the culprit has been found...'

'There is one snag though.' Judith was looking directly at Gerard Ruddler. 'Madame seems to feel that her Insurance Company should pay for this private man. Is that feasible?'

'I'm not certain. She's just changed her Company – and what their methods are I do not know.'

She had threatened to change; Judith remembered the letter waiting to be posted on the hall table, that must have contained the cancellation of the original policy. Trust Madame to have made things more complicated.

'I had better go up and talk to her, then try to contact the Paris office,' Gerard Ruddler decided.

But Judith put out a restraining hand. 'Before you go – I'd like to call a doctor in to see Madame, after this upset it would be only sensible for her to have a check-up. Have I your permission?'

'Will she not agree to that herself?'

'She hasn't done in the past – although most patients out of hospital have a follow-up visit from their G.P.'

'But who is my sister-in-law's local doctor these days?'

Marcelle Guis spoke. 'The one who treated her for the gall-bladder trouble prior to the operation is away ill at the moment; Rosa told me so the other day. You will have to seek the one Madame had before – Doctor Previne.'

'He and his partner have a surgery on the outskirts of the town. Would you like me to put a call through for you?' Surprisingly, this offer came from Garth. He made a move towards the study. 'I presume that, although it isn't exactly an emergency, you wish him to come as soon as possible?'

'Yes, please.' As she spoke, Judith felt Gerard Ruddler's hand press upon her arm.

'And do not worry, Judith,' he murmured comfortingly, 'if you receive any objection to the doctor's visit I shall shoulder all the blame.'

'He's a proper smoothie, that man,' Fenella remarked, accompanying her cousin into the kitchen afterwards.

'He only wants to do his best for his sole surviving relative,' Judith countered.

'Maybe. But I wish he'd go easy on your Christian name – Marcelle Guis was looking daggers, and you don't want any trouble from *her*. According to Paul – a long time ago she and Gerard Ruddler were lovers.'

'Do you think that's true?' But why shouldn't it be? Judith thought. Marcelle had shown jealousy and possessiveness before. She ought to have guessed.

'A mistress – even an ex-mistress – can be

a dangerous person to have around,' said a sagacious young Fenella, perching herself on the table to watch her cousin prepare a glass of squash for Madame to take with her evening tablet. 'Anyhow, this whole fracas has made a very sour ending to the afternoon. What do *you* reckon has happened to the ring?'

'I've no idea.' Judith shot her cousin a sideways glance. 'But until it's found everybody on the staff is suspect – you do realise that?'

'Yes, I suppose so.' Seemingly unperturbed, Fenella took out her make-up bag and relined her eyes. 'Who's your favourite in the "who-dun-it" stakes? It appears we all had the opportunity: Paul, Rosa, me, certainly Heinzmann and you.'

You've forgotten Garth, remember you said he was in the house this morning searching for Heinzmann?... Judith wondered what Fenella would have replied to that. Probably laughed with disbelief. I wish I could, Judith thought; just now, out in the hall, had Garth's offer to help been a front? Her forehead was disfigured by a contemplative frown.

And yet, she was thinking a moment later, why should his guilt or innocence be bothering her? It would be more rational to be concerned with her own reputation; for it was possible that in the eyes of others she was the present major suspect. The one who had had the most opportunity to carry out such a theft. Already, Marcelle Guis had dropped vague innuendoes. What if they were converted into straight accusations? Accusations which, tossed into the ready receptacle of Madame Ruddler's mind, might be difficult to refute.

Catching the sound of Marcelle Guis now questioning Rosa in the room next door and realising that as soon as a private detective turned up formal interrogation was something they might all have to get used to, she said to Fenella:

'By the way, where's Paul?'

'Oh, he disappeared immediately after lunch. He went to meet that American – to take him this month's repayment and to persuade him to wait for some of the rest until Paul starts to work again. They were meeting at Bordeaux – I think it was.'

'That's quite a long drive.'

'Yes. I expect they'll have drinks together and Paul will wake up tomorrow morning with one of his headaches.' Fenella was nonchalant. If she was disappointed that Paul hadn't been there to see her drive off with Garth after all she did not show it. To Fenella, Judith thought, that would be just the luck of the game. She envied her cousin's equanimity.

At seven o'clock, Doctor Previne arrived. He reminded Judith of the Abbé Sauvan; he had that same almost fatalistic air about him. It scarcely needed Judith to explain that he had been called without the patient's consent; but, on being ushered into the bedroom, he tactfully dealt with that problem:

'But why should I not decide to visit you, my dear Madame?' he smilingly demanded. 'Especially as I was passing here from another patient.'

'At this time of night?' Madame, since no-one in the house had cared to inform her in advance of the doctor's coming, glared in suspicious surprise.

'The sick do not watch the clock. Come now, Madame, I treated you for your heart condition in the past, did I not? So what is wrong if I wish to look up an old patient?'

'You medical men never do anything without some ulterior motive,' Madame answered drily. 'You're aware that I've recently returned from England, having undergone surgery?'

'*Mais oui.* I ran into the good Abbé Sauvan the other day and he mentioned it. I promised myself then that I would drop in when the chance came – and enquire how you are.'

There was a sniff. 'On the off-chance of finding me unwell so you can pick up a sizable fee, I've no doubt?' The doctor had his fingers on her wrist and was taking her pulse, but she was too busy talking to notice.

'As for that Father Sauvan – these village priests know too much of other people's business. They learn it through their confessional boxes...'

'How do you think Madame is?' Judith's query had had to wait until the end of the doctor's visit. They had come downstairs, she on the pretext of seeing him out, and had gone into the study.

He adjusted his thick-rimmed spectacles. 'As far as I can determine without a fuller examination, M'selle, she is not too bad. I agree she is in an excitable condition, but her heart-beat remains regular and fairly strong.'

Judith showed relief. She had, of course, already told him about the drama of the day. 'So I'll continue giving the heart tablets, the digoxin, as before?'

'Yes, I do not see any reason for an increased dosage. But I can prescribe some stronger sedative for the night-time if you ever feel it is necessary.'

'Thank you, that would be a help. It's kind of you take an interest at all in the circumstances.'

'Because Madame chose to consult another doctor for her gall-bladder trouble?' His throaty laugh rang out. 'That was not a novel move, Mademoiselle. Over the years Madame has called on almost every doctor in the province – and none of them ever completely satisfied her.'

Judith, glad that he had accepted the situation so philosophically, said: 'Yet you were the one to bring her through the cardiac attack over twenty months earlier, it seems?'

'I carried out the medical treatment, *oui*. But the nuns at the hospice in Lourdes must take the credit for her eventual recovery.'

'That must have been about the time her husband died?'

'Unfortunately, yes. She was still convalescing there when he suddenly collapsed.'

'He was your patient, too?'

'Well, I was called that night. But when I reached here there was nothing I could do. He was dying – of a – now what is the correct translation? – ah, yes, a massive aneurysm.'

'And what was the effect of his death on his wife? Was there any deterioration in her condition afterwards?'

'I do not really think so, though his going must have been a shock to her. However, she pulled herself together, came back to Villiers, hired a manager to keep the estate ticking over and seemed to lose little of her fire. The only pity was – I became a convenient scapegoat for her widowhood. For whenever she had anything wrong with her after that she made certain she consulted one of my colleagues instead.' He pulled a comical face. 'Madame, as you have doubtless deduced for yourself, Mademoiselle, can be a somewhat eccentric and revengeful lady. You must take care never to cross her...'

TWELVE

Mist veiled the countryside next morning, a thick unpleasant mist which pushed its way down the craggy mountainside, across the grounds, then swirled suffocatingly about the house. Indoors, the atmosphere was no more congenial. For one reason or another almost everybody was exhibiting some sign of tension – even though they were keeping these reasons private – and the theft of the ring, as if by some mute general consensus, was rarely mentioned – at least downstairs.

It was as if they were adopting the childish belief that if no-one alluded to the event it might magically fade away. But of course it didn't. Nor did the interlocking air of wariness between them.

'Typical week-end weather,' Garth commented tersely to Judith, meeting her in the passage-way by the kitchen around eleven o'clock. He seemed about to walk on but then, regarding her more closely, appeared to relent. 'You look tired... Did Madame keep you up till the early hours bemoaning her loss?'

'No.' She was ignoring his irony. 'As a matter of fact, with the help of light sedation, she went to sleep quite quickly.'

He made no reply to that. He was again on the look-out for Heinzmann who – judging by the noise some minutes before – had been flirting with Rosa somewhere at the rear of the house. '...where employees are usually to be found,' Marcelle Guis would probably have sarcastically pointed out – had she seen Garth's gum boots coming over the front step onto her highly-polished floor. Not that it would have made any impact. It wasn't likely that anyone at Villiers could have successfully ordered him to use the back – or servants' – entrance.

He wasn't that sort of man, Judith thought. His morning's work in the mist had left his hair damp, so that it lay close against his scalp. And her gaze traced the visible lines of the strong bones beneath.

'What about the doctor – is he coming again today?' he asked then.

'No.' Judith pulled her eyes away. 'He was willing to, but Madame doesn't seem to be too bad now. She's conferring with her brother-in-law at the moment, about the hiring of the private investigator.'

He nodded. Then, surprising her, said quietly: 'I presume none of this will stop you coming over to the cottage tonight?'

'Do you still want me to?' She stumbled a little. 'I imagined – because of our argument – the invitation might have been withdrawn.'

He gave her a lop-sided smile. 'Let's say we had a professional wrangle. But it shouldn't impinge on out-of-work relationships... And don't walk across this evening, I'll pick you up in the land-rover.'

Feeling rather awkward, Judith left the matter at that. The drift of uneasy suspicion that was moving through the house was widening the gap between them all. Marcelle Guis, pale and up-tight, publicly upbraided Rosa for egging Heinzmann on – and she, like the German, sank into a resentful silence. Even Fenella lost some of her ebullience.

As for Gerard Ruddler, he seemed too busy consoling and advising his sister-in-law to spare much thought for the anxieties of anyone else. During the morning he didn't come downstairs at all. And going into the dining-room for lunch, Judith heard from Fenella – haphazardly setting the table for one – that he had requested a meal in his room.

'It appears he's tired.' Fenella showed a conspicuous lack of sympathy. 'But after his hours of dancing attendance upstairs he oughtn't to be surprised.'

'He's been very kind to Madame,' Judith said. 'She's extremely grateful.' Sitting down, she re-arranged the carelessly-laid cutlery. 'Isn't Paul joining me either? I haven't had a sight of him since his trip to Bordeaux.'

'He's got a bit of a hangover. I took him a cup of tea earlier, but it wasn't very welcome.'

'Did he settle the car business satis-factorily?'

'It seems so. He managed to scrape together the instalment that's due now. But he was becoming rather desperate about the next few months'. However, after a few drinks, the American apparently became wonderfully reasonable – said as Paul wasn't working at present he'd wait a bit. So the heat's off.' As she spoke, Fenella opened the top drawer of the nearby sideboard, selected a napkin and tossed it across the table like a ball. Judith attempted to catch it but missed. And her cousin laughed. 'Butter-fingers!'

'I hope you won't do that with the soup when you bring it. Why are you doing this anyway? – it's usually Rosa's job.' Since Madame Drouet's departure Rosa had been doing a good deal of the cooking – although the housekeeper kept her under surveillance and when the food was ready liked to do the serving up herself. It enabled her to check on each dish, to prepare Madame Ruddler's tray personally – and left Rosa free to set the places in the dining-room then to wait at table.

Fenella shrugged. 'Because of this missing ring trouble the whole schedule's in a chaotic state. Marcelle Guis has hardly been in the kitchen at all this morning. She was in her room talking to Gerard Ruddler for quite a while. She set me dusting the upstairs corridor, so I overheard. Seems your admirer has come up with two or three ideas – for one thing, when this private detective turns up, Gerard Ruddler's going to propose a search.'

'Of our individual rooms?'

'I suppose it'll be of the whole house – plus the estate's other buildings. But I didn't catch anything else – Marcelle Guis must have remembered I was just outside, because at that point she turned round smartly and slammed the door.'

'You managed to get away then?...' Garth looked relieved when, at half-past eight that evening, Judith appeared on the front step and watched him driving up. She hadn't been able to change; but he was wearing, as if to create a good impression, a collar and tie for once. Against the white shirt, his fading summer tan looked attractively revitalised.

'Things worked out very nicely,' Judith told him, as they clattered off in the land-rover. 'Gerard Ruddler is taking his meal with Madame and keeping her company for an hour or so – and with Marcelle Guis anxious to give her services they obviously don't require me. I've told Paul where I can be contacted if any kind of emergency blows up.' She had come across him in the sitting-room, with his feet up on the settee, still looking seedy.

The interior of the cottage was unmodernised but quaint, with a kitchen leading off the tiny living-room and a bathroom of sorts at the back. Furnished with a drink, she was shown round.

'I'd extend your guided tour to the second floor – except you might get the wrong idea – and try to flee,' Garth said. And there was a grin at her spark of discomfiture.

Good-naturedly, she waited for a chance to retaliate. And, sitting beside him on a rickety sofa before the open stone fireplace later, she asked with exaggerated innocence: 'How did you enjoy your outing with Fenella yesterday?'

He was absent-mindedly swirling his whisky around his glass – and he glanced up quickly. But then, seeing the glint of mischief in her eyes, he smiled. 'I often go into town on a Friday – to the timber merchants – and when your cousin expressed a wish to go shopping and see the place by daylight I could hardly deny her a lift.'

Then he definitely hadn't used the outing as a petulant way of scoring a point after their argument? Fenella had been mistaken about that. I should have known myself, though, that he wouldn't be so petty ... she thought, with sudden warmth towards him.

He bent to put another log on the crackling fire for her benefit, and his hair showed up raven-black under the glow. Abruptly conscious of his physical presence, as she had once been on the boat coming out to France, she was disturbed to feel a shaft of answering femininity leap up to constrict her throat.

It felt like a pulse-beat then, at the side of her neck – rapid, strong – too strong. In an effort to forget it and the sensual feelings it was further engendering, she said in a rush:

'I have to congratulate you on your tidiness here.' She compared it with the often alarming state of her brother's quarters in hospital. But, hearing that, Garth threw back his head and laughed.

'I had a good clear-up in your honour,' he confessed. 'Ordinarily, I'm the least domesticated creature.'

As their time together drew on, they sat in companiable silence – watching the flames throw their light on the whitened stone of the hearth, casting colours on the glasses in their hands.

'Another drink?' he enquired softly.

But she shook her head. 'I shall soon have to go.'

'I'm sorry...' She felt his arm lying across the back of her shoulders then one hand moving to the nape of her neck... Her face was being turned towards his. And his mouth was seeking hers.

It was hard, forceful – and his fingers pressed into her hair.

After long, long moments she began to be frightened, not by his passion but, strangely, by her own. 'Please ... please...'

He drew away. 'I'm sorry. You're still nursing your wounds... I shouldn't have been so rough.' He was gentle again.

'It's just that...' she sought for words – and for breath, the place where his chest had pressed against her breast seemed to burn. '...that I must now return to my patient.'

'Of course.' He helped her to her feet. 'But you'll come again?'

Part of her would have said eagerly: 'Whenever you like...' But the other, the more controlled part, said primly: 'Why, yes – if Madame's progress permits.'

Paul peered out from the sitting-room as Garth escorted her back through Villiers' door. With Fenella unwillingly ensconced in the kitchen washing-up, he was glad to dispense with his boredom and to converse with someone.

'Coming in here for a few minutes?' he

asked the two of them.

But Judith shook her head. 'It's time for me to help Madame to bed.'

Paul's hopeful expression faded. He still looked rough, his navy sweater was crumpled and his hair unkempt 'You could do with an early night yourself,' Judith told him, in a sisterly fashion. 'I hear you returned very late last night?'

'Yes.' He smothered a yawn. 'It seems I missed quite a scene while I was away?'

'The one about the ring? Yes, it was quite nasty.'

'Madame Ruddler certainly knows how to practice the histrionics. It is foolish and not worth the cost – she will give herself another heart attack. She's plenty of other rings, hasn't she?'

'Yes, but she's determined to retrieve this particular one – and you can't blame her,' Judith said.

'And what's this about the possible arrival of some sort of private investigator? Is that true?'

'It seems so.' Judith's gaze covered both men. 'And if – or when – he comes, assuming Fenella is correct, there's going to be a thorough search of everyone's belongings.'

As the week-end passed into Monday she saw Garth several times. 'He does not come here so often in the past, that one,' Rosa remarked slyly in English, in Judith's hearing.

Judith said nothing – yet afterwards, thinking of the comment, found an insidious doubt creeping in about Garth's motives. To ascribe his more frequent calls at the house wholly to a growing attraction to herself might possibly be naive. She disliked herself for even considering it – but in the present circumstances couldn't he be dropping in to discover what was going on about the lost ring as well?

After all, it had been almost his first question on meeting her at the bottom of the stairs half an hour ago.

'No further developments on the missing property, I presume?'

'No, I desperately wish it was otherwise.' Standing on the second step, about to take up Madame's coffee, she had had the advantage of seeing directly into these deep-set eyes.

'Desperately?' One eyebrow had cocked at her choice of adverb. 'You're not being especially harassed, are you? The finger of suspicion shouldn't point more directly at you than at anyone else.'

'No, but I feel it does – for obvious reasons. I had more opportunity than anybody to remove that ring from Madame's room.' Ironically, considering these unpleasant speculations which had pushed themselves into her mind about the chances *he* might have had, she had found it a relief to share her strain. And the comfort of having another person show indignation on her behalf had had a measureable warmth – it had almost felt as if she were being encircled by his arms again.

'And what about the progress in the hiring of the private investigator?' she remembered he had asked then. Had he been sympathetic merely to pump her? How could one tell? 'When is he coming?'

'Tuesday I think.' The delay had been caused because Madame was still attempting to filter off the man's costs. But the fact that she had cancelled her previous Insurance policy before being officially accepted by the new company had left her caught between two stools, and the latter was refusing to pay. It had been left to her brother-in-law to try and unravel the mess – and, as he had told an enquiring Judith later, the week-end had complicated things still further...

'I do wish the police had been called in straightaway though,' Judith had said to Garth, after repeating Gerard Ruddler's story. 'It would have been best for everybody...' Except the thief, she had added – to herself.

Garth had looked thoughtful. 'So Tuesday is D-day – when we should all watch out for ourselves?'

'Well, one person should – the one who knows where that ring is at present.'

Doctor Previne made a final call on Madame during the late afternoon. But if her state ever warranted it, he assured Judith before leaving, he or his partner would always be available.

'In spite of the doubtful welcome we must anticipate,' he added, with a smile.

Nothing Judith did for her patient that evening seemed completely right. And, after she had settled her down for the night, she made for the sanctuary of her own room with a feeling of release.

But then, on opening the door, she blinked and started. The light was already on and Fenella was perched at the end of her bed.

'You gave me a fright,' Judith said, as she removed her uniform belt.

'Sorry, darling.' Coming to the end of the cigarette she was smoking, Fenella stubbed it out on the clean china ash-tray on the nearby table. 'But I guessed you wouldn't be too long so decided to wait. I want to borrow some shampoo, I meant to buy some the other day in Lourdes – but forgot. I did have a large bottle but it's back amongst my things in San Sebastian.'

Judith rolled up her belt, but about to deposit it on the dressing-table paused. A tin of talcum powder was lying on its side and that section of the dressing-table top was covered in a film of the stuff.

'Don't blame that mess on me,' Fenella remarked, watching Judith's fleeting frown. 'It was like that when I came in; I daresay when you last went out the door slammed and caused a draught that sent the tin over.'

Judith, wondering if that was likely, began searching for the asked-for shampoo. She was certain she had brought at least three sachets with her from England and so far had used only one. But where the other two had got to she couldn't discover. She looked twice through all the drawers and cupboards and then, mystified, gave up.

'By the way, Fenella,' she said, as her cousin eventually made to leave, 'do you intend to remain at Villiers until Madame Drouet returns? Or haven't you decided yet?'

'Oh, I'm not in a roaring hurry,' was the languid reply. 'For the moment Paris can wait.'

Judith was about to climb into bed when she remembered the silk inside-pocket of her empty case. That was the only place where she hadn't looked for the sachets. Curious to learn if her sudden hunch was right, she padded – barefoot – across to the wardrobe, stood on a chair, and lifted the case down. Carrying it across to the bed, she opened the unlocked lid and felt inside the ruche pocket.

Yes, the sachets were there – plus something else. Surprised to find her fingers closing on a hard circular object, she drew it out.

For a second her mind didn't register. And the ring, meanwhile, rested on the palm of her hand – with its three glittering diamonds fixed on her face like triple glass eyes inquisitively waiting for her reaction.

Dazedly, Judith stared at it – her belated gasp of astonishment sweeping coldness into her mouth. Although she had never really seen it before – Madame was too careful an owner to gratify the gaze of the casual onlooker – it went without saying that it must be her employer's.

But what was it doing here? Here in her room, in her case? Someone must have been in and planted it. But why? Why did someone want to incriminate her in the theft?

And who, in this contrasting little group of people around her, could it be?

THIRTEEN

Still holding the ring, Judith sat down weakly on the bed, taking the place vacated by Fenella a short time before. The remembrance of her cousin jerked at her. Could

125

Fenella have possibly done this?

Perhaps I almost caught her in the act? Judith conjectured; she heard my footsteps, swung back after quickly returning the case to the top of the wardrobe and was unlucky enough to knock over the talcum powder.

Yet Fenella, puffing away at her cigarette, hadn't appeared flustered. She'd been her usual nonchalant self – and a bit bored with waiting. Besides, juggling with suspicions about a member of one's own family wasn't pleasant.

I'll watch how she acts towards me tomorrow, Judith determined, after the ring has been returned to its rightful owner. I'll watch how they all act... Though just how the ring was going to be returned was another problem. She could hardly confront Madame Ruddler with: 'Look what I've found in my case! Isn't it extraordinary?'

No-one would accept that explanation. After it, arrest would probably be inevitable. There was only one thing for it – the ring had to be put back into its owner's keeping in the same way it had been removed – secretly, without anyone else knowing. But to do it successfully would be difficult.

Tense and worried, Judith made no effort to sleep. When should she try and carry out her plan? To sneak into Madame's bedroom and return the ring now was too risky. One stumble and just enough noise to rouse her patient and she would be plunged into a very tricky situation – standing there with the incriminating evidence in her hand. And in any event where was the best place in the bedroom to leave the ring? Cupboards, drawers, vases, chairs – there didn't seem to be anywhere that had not been thoroughly searched – in some cases several times over. No, the ring had to turn up in a spot never thought of before.

But where?... It was a problem that begged to be solved before daybreak. But it wasn't.

At six a.m. Madame Ruddler awoke and rang her handbell. 'Will you help me to the bathroom, Nurse?' she said. 'And while I'm in there I'd like you to straighten my bed, please – the bottom sheet has creases as deep as plough furrows.'

'All right,' Judith promised. 'And I'll make up the fire as well.'

Raking through the embers, attempting to encourage life into a few smoking pieces of coal, she couldn't stop thinking of the ring back in her own room. Wasn't this the time, while Madame was absent, to slip out and fetch it? This was the sort of opportunity that might not come again. Apart from the light in the corridor the rest of the house still lay in curtained semi-darkness and no-one else was yet about.

She simply had to return the ring now, this moment. And that vital question of where to leave it so that eventually she could pretend to find it again needed an answer immediately...

'The trouble was, Nurse, you couldn't have been cleaning this room of mine thoroughly enough,' Madame Ruddler was stating loudly three hours later. 'I'm sure if you had you'd have nosed out this ring long before today. And think of the fuss we'd have been saved. Don't you agree, Gerard?... And you, Madame Guis?'

Of course, they had both been summoned immediately to hear the news. But it was Marcelle Guis who shot Judith the queerest glance. 'You say you came upon the ring lodged in the curve of the hearth just here, Nurse?'

'That's right, underneath the brass fender. It must have rolled there – just as Madame, having finished the check on her jewels that day, closed the box.'

'But what made you consider looking in this spot today?'

'It was a matter of luck the fender was moved this morning. When Herr Heinzmann brought in the coal scuttle I took it from him – and on shifting in into position afterwards I happened to knock the fender out of place.' The lies she was having to tell made Judith hot.

The whole episode had been such a strain: the hurrying back down the corridor with the ring in her hand while Madame was still in the bathroom earlier on; its concealment beneath the fender after the idea had come to her – then the interminable hours of waiting for a suitable opening, so that the charade of the sudden 'discovery' of the lost ring could begin.

Even by lunch-time she had not recovered. As on the occasions when she met anyone else and had to face their inevitable questions, she felt that the deception she had carried out must be emblazoned across her face.

Word of the finding of the ring had spread around the other occupants like a wind-raised fire. Most displayed some sort of relief; even Rosa looked less disgruntled; and Fenella burst out with an apparently genuine: 'Well, thank the Lord that's turned up! Now we can forget the tiresome thing.'

It was Gerard Ruddler who informed Garth. Judith came across them in the doorway of the study – Garth, a roll of accounts in his hand, looking as if he were going in to do some paperwork.

'I am just repeating the gist of what happened, Judith,' Gerard Ruddler explained. 'The welcome – if surprising – finale to our plight.'

'You've cancelled the visit of the private detective, I take it?' Garth asked.

'*Oui*. My sister-in-law naturally asked me

to do that straightaway.'

Garth lingered with Judith after the Frenchman had gone. 'I don't expect your find brought you much glory from our boss, did it?' he drily observed. 'I'm afraid she's not the type to show enormous gratitude.'

'No – but by rights she ought to give Judith a reward...' The interjecting voice was Paul's. He was coming from the direction of the stairs to join them. 'Anyhow, the rest of us can thank you, Judith...' he said lightly. 'A load's been lifted off everybody's back by the solving of this enigma.'

Enigma – or whatever one called it, Judith thought afterwards, the mystery of the ring had hardly been 'solved'. On the contrary, for her it had disturbingly deepened. Some-one, as yet unidentified, had stolen that ring and then had foisted it on her. *Why?* she wondered yet again.

Originally, it must have been one of those 'impulse' thefts – a chance seen – then seized. But had the disposal of the property, its conversion into cash, turned out to be more difficult than anticipated, risky in a town like Lourdes? Perhaps so. And perhaps the final straw, causing the decision to give up and dump the evidence, had been the coming rumoured search... Everyone had known of it, of course. She had even informed Garth and Paul herself.

She scrutinized them all in her mind:

Garth, who had threatened to obtain money somehow: and Paul, who had needed it to pay off his car, until the American had turned out to be so reasonable. Then there was Heinzmann – a drinking man, and heavy drinkers never seemed to have sufficient cash. They could all be suspects.

Then there was another possibility altogether ... that someone had, not jettisoned the ring in a bit of a panic, but had deliberately planted it. Not out of fright – but out of premeditated malice. Someone coolly planning to plunge her into trouble, to get her branded as a thief – and see her dismissed.

A person, in essence, her enemy. Resentful of her presence; perhaps foolishly jealous. And only one had ever shown that sort of emotion towards her: Marcelle Guis.

FOURTEEN

Outside Villiers – and now inside... It seemed to Judith that everywhere there was a slow uncanny build-up of something very frightening. It had always been hard to forget, especially on her walks, that out there, in that autumn-cast countryside, was a man – or woman – who had profited from the blackmailing of her patient. Somehow the knowledge of that had always thrown a shadow across the beauty. Even her hikes to the remoter reaches of the mountain track had in some sense been despoiled.

But that had been an external menace – a past occurrence – and to someone else. This, though perhaps on a different plane, was a present threat – to herself. And there was nothing she could do about it. The stolen ring had been returned – and, fortuitously, she had escaped that trouble – or trap. But would she be left alone from hereon? That was the alarming question?...

Once the ring lay safely in the jewel-box again Madame Ruddler was all for having the key back on her person. For a couple of days she had it dangling from her bracelet but as it got in the way when she took her meals she decided to return it to her neck.

A replacement for the broken chain was ordered from one of the shops and arrangements were made for Judith to go into Lourdes to collect it when Garth made his next business trip.

It turned out to be a grey sort of day. A few hardy pilgrims were making their way to the Basilicas; but in the little bistro near the river where Garth suggested having a warming drink not another foreigner was to be seen.

'This is the time of year when Lourdes is

returned to the French,' Garth commented. 'They'll see she recuperates – and come next Easter she'll be bursting at the seams again.'

Even the middle of the town was quiet. And while Garth went to call on various merchants, she stopped off at the market square, picked up Madame's silver chain, then went back across the river and spent a quarter of an hour browsing around a book shop.

She had just come out onto the narrow pavement and was walking down the road, studying the guide-book she had bought, when she heard the clatter of a car racing round a corner behind her. Immediately, there was a warning shout.

'M'selle! M'selle!...' The cry came from a shopkeeper hanging an advertising placard in his door. There followed such a flurry of French that even the more proficient linguist, Fenella, would have been hard put to roughly translate.

But the meaning, transcending language, was literally bursting out of the excited words: Move! Move! Don't waste time looking round – but move...

After that, she did not stop to think – but obeyed like an automaton, jumping to the back of the pavement, coming up hard against the iron railings and stumbling to the side to her knees.

Meanwhile, the car behind her was careering on, swerving into the opposite kerb and disappearing round the next corner.

'*Mon Dieu!...*' The shopkeeper had raced towards her.

Judith was picking herself up. 'I'm all right. Don't worry... *Merci.*' She tried to smile into his anxious face.

'That maniac!' Hearing her English, he abandoned his French. 'Either he is drunk – or he is a terrible driver. Coming at that speed down these narrow byways – he left himself no room to negotiate the corners... You wish me to call a gendarme?'

'I don't think there's any use. He'll be back on the main road by now.'

'The car was big, black. A pity, but I did not note the number nor the make.'

It doesn't matter, Judith thought, I know it. It had been Madame's saloon – and Heinzmann, by himself, had been at the wheel.

'But you must be trembling all over, M'selle.' Her newfound friend was regarding her with concern. 'Would you like to rest awhile in my shop?'

'It's kind of you – but I'll be all right to go on,' she assured him. 'And I'm due to meet someone by the Grotto about now.'

Directed to take the shortest route, she emerged on the opposite side to the Grotto's compound and saw the land-rover already parked across the way. But Garth wasn't in it – he was speaking to the driver of the vehicle in front. It was the saloon from Villiers.

Judith quickened her steps – but before she could reach them she saw Heinzmann nod, wind up his window, then pull off.

Something prevented her from mentioning her near-accident as they started home. Instead, as the land-rover laboured up the first hill, she said casually: 'I thought I caught sight of Herr Heinzmann in town…'

'He's been here, so you may have done.'

'Oh, you knew he was coming?'

'Yes. Ruddler asked if I would mind his sending Heinzmann on an errand some time – he wanted shirts and stuff to be taken in to be laundered before he returns to Paris. So I thought today would be a good choice – as I wouldn't be around to supervise the work on the estate.'

He paused to change gear as the land-rover hissed its resistance to the climb. 'Actually, Heinzmann passed by a few minutes ago – and stopped to have a word. It looked to me as if he'd also stopped off to have a few drinks … so I told him to drive straight home.'

The sunless day seemed even duller on their return journey. It hadn't seemed to matter on their way out. Sitting beside Garth, chatting about normal things, she had felt the unpleasant happenings at Villiers fade further into the background. But the incident of the car had been not only a physical intrusion – churning up her inside and leaving her utterly shaken – it had forced back upon her mind before time, as it were, the house and all its occupants.

In a sense, was her thought, it's proved that little by little I'm losing any chance even of mental release.

It startled her when Garth, taking advantage of a stretch of deserted road, suddenly leant across and touched her clasped, gloveless hands.

'You seem in quite a brown study,' he murmured. 'There's nothing wrong, is there?'

Yes, there's, a great deal...The words came involuntarily to the tip of her tongue. But then abruptly, that same inner caution that had so far kept her from telling him of the car episode, surged forward and sliced them off.

'I'm sorry...' was her lame excuse. 'It's this enervating weather.'

'You say Gerard Ruddler's going back to Paris?' Her remark came as they were turning into the drive.

'Yes, he's thinking of going at the beginning of next week. You didn't know?'

She shook her head.

'It seems he has to deal with the wages of

his man servant and daily help – and there are various bills to be settled in person. I daresay he'll come back eventually.'

'Yes, I expect so.'

She sensed Garth regarding her reflectively as they parted at the house. But all he said was: 'If you ever want to go into town on your own behalf – you know I'll only be too pleased to take you.'

She did not have much opportunity to speak to Gerard Ruddler alone till next afternoon – when they converged in the hall. They were both dressed to go out – he in formal attire, sharp creases to his beautifully-cut suit and a glitter to his silver-tipped cane, and she in trousers and anorak.

'Ah, Judith, it is you … is it possible for me to give you a lift. I am going into town to collect my laundry – it is supposed to be a twenty-four-hour service, so I shall be putting it to the test.'

'Are you using Madame's car?'

'Today I am hiring one from the village. I do not care to take Herr Heinzmann away too often, he is wanted here.'

'It's a pity you can't drive yourself.'

'Yes, it is sometimes tiresome. But it seems beyond my capabilities to deal with mechanical objects – I have never been a practical man. Anyhow, I would be charmed to have you share this car.'

'That's kind of you – but all I need is some

exercise. And my usual trek up to the footbridge will give me that.'

Looking down on her, he smiled. 'You are still enamoured of the view? I have not been up there for years, so I have almost forgotten what it is like.'

'I'd suggest your coming along one day and refreshing your memory,' she said lightly, 'except that I hear from Garth Massingham you're considering returning to Paris? Madame doesn't yet know?'

'*Non* – I shall inform her in a day or two when my arrangements are complete.'

As the hired car drew him away, he gave his friendly debonair wave. And as Judith walked off in the opposite direction he remained on her mind. She hoped Madame Ruddler wouldn't be upset at this, his second departure – though she must know better than anyone in the house, excepting perhaps Marcelle Guis, that no matter how long her brother-in-law remained at Villiers he was unlikely to become a countrified man. He was too much the City type, urbane, fastidious, the connoisseur, the gourmet – more at home in Monte Carlo or Rome – with exclusive clubs, casinos, luxurious hotels or his own expensive apartment on the Left Bank at hand.

It was frustrating, but that day she had to turn back long before reaching the footbridge. Yesterday's clouds of mists had rolled closer, obscuring the gully and crags – and it wasn't safe to go on.

Garth and Heinzmann were about as she walked down the track towards the outbuildings again. She heard the latter's voice first. Then, on rounding a corner of the garage, she saw them standing together. Heinzmann had one hand stretched out, palm uppermost, and Garth appeared to be counting money into it.

Judging by his frown, he was doing so with a certain reluctance. 'I can't manage more now, this will have to suffice,' she heard him say curtly. Then, inadvertently having spoken in English in the heat of the moment – as she had heard him do once before, he corrected himself and continued in German. Heinzmann, plainly less than satisfied, growled back. But Garth was adamant. 'Nein, nein...'

The monetary transaction, whatever it was about, made Judith instinctively draw back out of sight until it was finished. Why was he paying Heinzmann? she wondered. It couldn't have been his wages – like everyone else's on the estate they were paid out each Friday – and today was only Tuesday.

When she next peered round the corner the two men had separated. And as Garth strode away he was replacing his wallet in his back trouser-pocket. The movement must have dislodged the other contents, for something had already fluttered to the ground.

It was a small, faded photograph. Picking it up a few seconds later, Judith saw it was quite old; the clothing worn by the sitter reminded her of family snaps of her mother's – taken in the thirties. The man here looked to be about thirty then – which meant he must now be very elderly.

Wondering if he could be a relative of Garth's, she scrutinized the bearded face but could discern no definite resemblance.

Since Garth was now nowhere to be seen, she took the photograph to her room when she got back – slipping it, for safe keeping, between the stiff covers of her passport in her shoulder-bag. As soon as possible, she would return it.

It came as a surprise when, on his arrival from town, Gerard Ruddler announced his intention to travel to Paris that very evening. 'I called in the station to enquire about future bookings,' he explained, 'and they mentioned a specially fast express going through tonight – with a first-class couchette available... It seems a pity to miss it.'

His sister-in-law, about to taste a bunch of grapes he had brought back for her, stopped. 'You're off tonight, Gerard!' She was astonished – then glum. 'You'll be coming back, I hope?'

'But naturally, my dear. And if you should happen to need me urgently, Madame Guis or Nurse here' – when it came to names he still abided by the formalities in Madame's presence – 'can telephone at once.'

'Heinzmann's been ordered to run Gerard Ruddler into the station tonight,' Fenella told Judith later in the kitchen. 'Rosa's a bit annoyed – it'll mean they'll probably have to break their date.'

'Is Rosa his steady girl friend now?' Judith asked.

'Well, I suppose they're having some sort of affair – though I doubt Heinzmann has sole possession. Rosa may live in this outback but she's as emancipated as any women's "libber"...'

'Promiscuity isn't liberty,' Judith pointed out, then – as so often when dealing with Fenella – felt like an elderly prude. Especially when there was a teasing laugh.

'Rosa takes while she can, darling. You can't blame her.'

'Perhaps not – but I should have thought Heinzmann had enough to do, keeping up with the demands of his thirst, let alone those of an avaricious young female.'

'Yes, his expenses may be heavy – but he's always on the look-out for ways of making extra money, shooting and such like. I bet he'd tackle anything if the reward was good enough.' Supposed to be cleaning the silver in the dining-room, Fenella collected the necessary cloths. But then, moving off, she thought of something else: 'Incidentally, in a round-about way I spoke to Rosa about that blackmailing matter.'

'You never told her?' Judith was horrified.

'No, I didn't come out with it as baldly as that. I just casually pumped her about the history of Madame's late husband. Asked if she'd ever heard anything. She said some old man once told her that long ago it was rumoured in the village that he'd spent a good deal of the Occupation years in Paris, collaborating with the Nazis in crooked art deals. But nothing was ever proved ... so over the decades everybody seems to have forgotten – or forgiven – it.'

Not everybody, Judith said grimly to herself.

Her cousin's lively mind seemed to pick up the thought, for she said with sudden expectancy: 'You've not ferreted out any more facts from Madame Ruddler?'

Judith shook her head. 'No – and perhaps I never shall.'

'Oh, don't dash my hopes of more secrets and skeletons in the cupboard coming out. I'm not losing my faith in your professional charisma yet.'

Her brother-in-law having departed. Madame lapsed into a low, irritable state. Doing without her usual nap next afternoon, she had Judith running about quite unnecessarily. I ought to insist she starts going downstairs again, Judith mused, it might give her something else to think about. But that day and the day following she cravenly avoided the issue – and what would inevitably turn out to be a protracted argument. St. Vincent's, she drily observed to Fenella, would have been ashamed of her lack of authority over a patient.

'Oh, let her stay where she is – in her room,' was Fenella's advice. 'We've enough trouble down here with Marcelle Guis prowling about and criticising...'

'I haven't come across her much since Gerard Ruddler left. Where is she this afternoon?'

'In town. Shopping. Paul drove her in.'

She hadn't seen Garth either, Judith then reflected. But he couldn't have missed the photograph yet – or he surely would have enquired at the house. Wanting to return it personally and regretting the lack of opportunity, she determined that no matter what happened she would slip out next day to try and find him.

Madame Ruddler, afternoon tea at hand, was sitting huddled in front of the bedroom fire as she left. She was frowning at a pile of papers sent in earlier by her accountants.

'They seem extraordinarily pernickety this year,' she growled. 'We've been through all these bills before.'

'Perhaps they want to make doubly sure

you agree with the final figures?' Judith suggested, feeling warmly disposed to their cautiousness, since their action was enabling her to take a short respite. No doubt they had learnt to check and recheck with Madame long before this, she was that sort of client.

When she couldn't find him anywhere else, Judith walked across to Garth's cottage. The door was unlocked. But after a couple of abortive knocks and just to make certain the place was empty, she glanced through the window.

On her previous visit, he had confessed he had tidied up specially for her – and today the state of the living-room bore him out. Quelling her feminine instinct to go in and give it a quick going-over in his absence, then biting back a smile on picturing his reaction, she returned to Villiers. Long-standing bachelors were apt to recoil from unsolicited female interference.

Rosa was dallying in the hall when she entered. There were letters on the table beside her. 'More mail has arrived?' Judith commented. 'Is there anything interesting?'

Rosa's face was expressionless. 'There are two things for you – and one for Madame Ruddler.'

'Then I'll take the latter up with me now.'

Judith's own correspondence consisted of a card from her brother, Roger, and the usual list of maternal advice from their mother. Her employer's letter, she noticed, bore a Lourdes postmark. And Madame, still sitting by the fire, began to tear at the envelope without so much of a glance at the writing as soon as it was delivered.

'There was a telephone call from my brother-in-law while you were out, Nurse,' she said, as she did so. 'And because you and Madame Guis weren't about Rosa answered. She never dreamt of putting it through to my extension, of course, but merely took a garbled message.'

'I'm sorry.' It was simpler to apologise than to argue one's case. 'Is the M'sieur going to ring again tonight?'

'No, tomorrow evening – if Rosa is to be believed. About half-past eight.' The mutilation of the delivered envelope had finished; one page of thin white paper was extracted and straightened out.

Madame began to read, fixing her reading glasses on the bridge of her nose. Near to her outstretched feet the fire crackled. And Judith reached for the poker and pushed a piece of coal further to the back.

Then, glancing again at her patient, she was suddenly still. 'Is something wrong, Madame?...'

There was no reply. 'Madame?' Judith repeated anxiously.

The other was slumped in her chair like a

huge Henry Moore figure, face drained of colour, body curves of stone.

'What a naive fool I have been!...' The murmur that eventually came was like a strangled echo thrown from another woman's throat. 'I should have guessed there would be another demand in time ... that the one in the spring would *not* be the last.'

Judith had stiffened. 'A demand, Madame!...'

But her words were cut off. Madame's head had jerked back – and regret for her own impulsive remarks was closing over her eyes like two black shutters. 'I would like you to leave me, Nurse...'

'But can't I do anything?' Judith's tone was pleading. 'If this communication is something to do with you being blackmailed again...'

'I erred in blurting anything out in the first instance,' was the heated interruption. 'And now, if it's starting up once more, outside interference is the last thing I want.'

'But Madame...'

'No, Nurse. I must deal with this in my own way.'

Judith gave a distraught glance backwards as she made to close the door. Her patient, crouching forward in her chair, was tearing the newly-arrived letter into shreds – and feeding it, scrap by scrap, into the flames of the bedroom fire.

FIFTEEN

Judith's self-reproof afterwards was bitter. She, like her patient, should have realised all along that the blackmailing wasn't over. Books, films, real-life court cases ... didn't they all throw up the same valid warning? – that blackmailers, with their evil and enticing 'final' demands, their 'just pay this last, bigger, sum and you'll be free of me for ever', rarely meant it?

They hammered away on fears, tortured nerves, raised false hopes – and continued to bleed their victim till dry. And this case probably would be no different. It would go on and on until some sort of crisis point was reached.

Madame Ruddler, mumbling frequently, had a restless night; and when she woke ate but a meagre breakfast. It was mid-morning when Judith, bringing in her coffee, found her finishing a telephone call – obviously to her bank. And it was then that she broke the news of her coming outing.

'Please inform Heinzmann, Nurse, that at one o'clock this afternoon I shall require the car.'

'You're not going out?' Judith was

astonished – and instantly perturbed.

'I must.'

'But how far are you thinking of going?'

'To town. To pick up some money. And I prefer to go alone.'

So this must be the outcome of yesterday's letter? Whatever orders it had contained – they clearly were going to be complied with. In some way cash was going to be paid out.

Judith's growing resolve was like hardening cement. 'A sudden outing like this might make you feel quite weak, Madame. You're so unprepared – and I insist on escorting you.'

There was a brief controversy. But because the older woman seemed to have little fight left in her Judith won a comparatively effortless victory.

At the requested time, she and Heinzmann assisted their employer outside and into the car. The instructions were precise. Heinzmann was to drive straight to the Rue de Bernadette, head for the bank – and park at the back entrance, not the front.

Marcelle Guis, dutifully seeing her mistress off and translating her words into German so that Heinzmann fully understood, stepped back as Judith climbed in beside Madame and closed the door. What she felt about the projected excursion Judith couldn't tell.

The journey passed in an uneasy silence.

Madame stared morosely out of the window, scarcely bothering even to nod when Judith enquired about her comfort. Not that any passenger of Heinzmann's could ever completely relax; his driving was too erratic and the condition of the car didn't help.

It had been raining in Lourdes and the streets were wet. Heinzmann wound his way through a maze of old buildings at the back of the market place then pulled up in a tiny cobbled square.

'I suppose you didn't bring any of my pills?' Madame asked. 'I need something for a headache.'

'Actually, I've provided for every contingency,' Judith was able to reply with a touch of satisfaction. 'And I've plenty of aspirins. There's even a flask of water so you can swallow them all right.'

Unfortunately, the bottle containing the tablets had slipped right down to the bottom of her shoulder bag, and after a fumbling attempt to locate it Judith was forced to remove some of the contents. Her passport came first – and out of it slipped the photograph she still hadn't returned to Garth.

'Who's that?' Madame said listlessly, picking it off the seat where it had fallen and squinting at the face.

'I'm not sure,' Judith answered, her groping finally rewarded. 'I found it in the grounds one afternoon...' She was about to add that it belonged to Garth Massingham when something about the way it was being studied made her hesitate. 'Is it someone you know, Madame?'

Her charge raised one hand to her eyes as if to shade them from the sun. 'I cannot be sure – it is over thirty years since...' Puzzled, she shook her head and then absent-mindedly tossed the photograph onto the car's window-shelf behind her. 'Oh, well – it is not important now.'

Heinzmann was already walking round to open the passenger door. Madame, grabbing Judith's proffered arm, heaved herself out. Then, pulling her fur coat closer against her, she straightened and gestured with her walking-stick.

'My business will take about half-an-hour, Nurse. You may see me through the rear entrance there – and afterwards perhaps you'll go and buy me a copy of the London Times somewhere? I'll pay you later...'

The worry Judith felt on being forced to allow her patient out of sight kept her tense. And once the small errand had been accomplished she found it impossible to wait in the car. Especially as a chain-smoking Heinzmann was leaning negligently across the bonnet. After a while spent watching her passers-by and several other customers using the Bank's rear door, she could endure the situation no longer.

'I'm going for a quick walk around the block,' she said, caring little that the German probably didn't have a clue as to her intention. He didn't seem bothered – he blew a couple of smoke rings and nodded.

Walking briskly, she left the square and went down the street at the side of the bank. The front of the buildings stood on a main road and the afternoon traffic was heavy. Pausing at the corner, the swish of passing wheels sending out sprays of old rain-water into the kerb by her feet, she noticed a taxi – its indicator light on the blink – waiting across the road for a chance to slip through the oncoming vehicles and drive over to this side.

There was a woman sitting close against the window in the back, her figure a furry blur, but her white distinctive profile sharp and clear behind the glass. It was Madame Ruddler's.

Judith's start of surprise and a natural desire to keep out of sight came together. So Madame hadn't been only to the bank, she had gone on to pay a second call? And it couldn't have been to a place very far away. The time factor proved that. She must have completed her financial business, asked one of the bank clerks to get her a taxi, then left almost immediately – through the front entrance.

But why had she gone? There could have been just one reason. She had not only collected the blackmail money today, she had delivered it as well. And she must have done it according to the letter's instructions, secretly, leaving the cash at some collection-address – as she had revealed she had done in the past.

Now, on her return, she was obviously going to walk through the bank once more, emerge through the same rear door – and hope to give the impression she had been in there the whole time.

Realising she had better return to the car herself, and be seen to be waiting, Judith hurried back.

She felt a growing solicitiousness as she tucked the rug around her employer's legs again. The other's face was drawn, with small lines of exhaustion dragging at the corners of her mouth. 'I hope you haven't overdone things on your first trip out, Madame?'

'Why should you think that withdrawing some money and checking my last few statements should have taxed me that much?' was the quick – and possibly suspicious – retort. 'I'm all right, Nurse.'

On the drive out Madame has been gloomy and introspective. Now she was edgy, and her nerves might have been electrified wires jangling beneath her skin. But to Judith she

152

said nothing more, even when the former –
looking out of the window as they reached
the river by the shrine – suddenly exclaimed:
'Look! Isn't that the estate's landrover and
Mr. Massingham?'

Today Madame wasn't interested in the
coming and goings of her employees though.
And as the landrover disappeared up a side
road only Judith's thoughts followed it.

It wasn't unusual for Garth to be here in
town, she acknowledged that. Yet it was as if
the sight of something and someone from
Villiers had signalled the opening of a pit in
her subconsciousness. And out of the
blackness unwanted queries seemed to be
slithering like a plague of suddenly-released
snakes.

Two days ago, an anonymous letter –
demanding and threatening – had been
posted in this town. Posted by whom?... That
was the frightening question. Up to this
moment she had never thought of anyone at
Villiers – but now the idea cut like a scalpel,
releasing the passage for more vipers.

Marcelle Guis had been in Lourdes that
particular afternoon. As had Paul... And what
of Garth? And even Heinzmann? Where had
they been? She remembered how the house
and surroundings had been exceptionally
quiet that day – almost empty of people.

It had to be faced anybody in Madame's
employment could be doing this black-

mailing ... was her next unwelcome thought. Why not? Perhaps the rumour of the collaborationist activities of Madame's husband hadn't died – as Rosa had thought. Perhaps somebody in the house had come to hear of it too – and had then come upon some kind of proof. Or enough evidence to act as a goad – an extortioner's goad. To wield as they saw fit.

And today, at the same hour as the demand for money had been acceded to, Garth had been glimpsed coming into town... Was his arrival just a coincidence?

Hating all such thoughts, but unable to suppress them, Judith sat as silent as Madame Ruddler. It hadn't occurred to her before, but in a sense she and the woman beside her both lay under a threat. Totally unconnected ones, of course.

Or were they?... This new conjecture flashed into her brain like a meteorite – and wouldn't be dislodged.

She already knew she had some kind of opponent in Villiers, a hidden someone who had probably planned to pitch her into disgrace and a subsequent dismissal as a thief. But up to this instant the motive of that person had been a riddle. Judith had mainly considered a possible jealousy: the jealousy of Marcelle Guis; the vestigial possessiveness of an old flame.

But what if the position was far more

serious than that? And linked in a definite way to Madame's?

What if there was another reason for wanting to be rid of her?... Not simple sexual jealousy at all. But a gnawing dread that she knew too much – too much about Madame Ruddler's blackmail...

But how could anyone in the house have discovered that Madame had told her anything? That was Judith's next tormented question. For a few dragging seconds, she sat nonplussed.

Then, abruptly, she recalled the morning she had weakened and spoken to Fenella. She re-heard her disbelieving cousin's phrases echoing through the empty kitchen: 'Blackmailed!... You're joking!' and the rest of their talk.

And she remembered – now with an icy shudder – that fateful crack in the door behind them. Someone must have been listening in. Fenella's fervently-expressed hope that Judith would eventually learn a great deal more had been so audible: 'Patients do tend to carry on confiding in their nurses... Keep on providing her with suitable openings...'

It has made it sound as if the raking out of further facts was to be Judith's prime intention.

The fear that had begun to move in Judith's heart must have been akin to that which had rumbled through their unknown eaves-dropper that morning, she thought. One revealed fact was always a rung up to another; and at the top of the ladder would be the last fact: the identity of Madame Ruddler's blackmailer.

It seemed so clear now. To prevent her ever learning their name that person wanted her out of Villiers. Wanted her to leave at the earliest possible moment. Even if that meant their using any method...

Memory pitched forward then the episode of the near-accident to herself in Lourdes – then Heinzmann – who, according to Fenella, would tackle any sort of job for extra money... And hard on the heels of that was a picture of Garth paying cash into his upturned palm. Garth, who had admitted to choosing to send the German into Lourdes that day – and who had known of her intention to search for a guide-book in that part of the town. Had he set it up? Had Heinzmann been paid to incapacitate – or scare – her?

The arteries of her scalp felt dilated – as if every fearful question she has posed during the journey had sent another spurt of adrenalin into her head. But I shan't go from this place, was her eventual shaky verdict; I can't allow myself to be forced from here – not until my job is finished.

But would the intimidation – if that was

what it was – continue? Could she expect any further incident? From a personal point of view, that was the most frightening question of all.

SIXTEEN

Judith took the expected telephone call from Gerard Ruddler that evening herself. 'I'm afraid you won't be able to speak to Madame tonight,' she apologised. 'She's asleep. I've given her a tablet.'

'So early?' The pause was reflective. 'Is she not well?'

'She's had an acute headache.'

'You sound worried, Judith…'

'I am rather. She went to town today and the outing might have been too much for her. But she insisted on going.'

'To town? Just straight there and back?'

'Well, we went to the bank.' She had hesitated, wondering if she should take this chance of passing some of the responsibility on, of telling Gerard Ruddler what was really happening. But confiding in Fenella had been a mistake – especially here in the house, where the walls themselves now seemed to have ears. She ought not to fall into that trap again.

'You said "we", Judith,' Gerard Ruddler was continuing. 'Does that mean you accompanied her?'

'But of course – though I had to force myself on her.'

'And did you remain with her the whole time?'

'Not exactly; she carried out her actual business alone.'

'Then she went into the bank by herself?'

'She wanted it that way.' It puzzled her as to where his questions were leading. 'Herr Heinzmann and I stayed with the car at the back.'

'Ah, I see... It is only that I am speculating on the possibility of the headache having been brought on by her mental attitude. I wondered if she started arguing in the bank, disputed the state of her accounts or something – she never trusts people in banks.'

'You're thinking of a psychological rather than a physical cause?'

'*Oui* – but it is just an idea, tossed out by a layman. I hope you do not take offence, Judith?'

'Of course not – and you may be right,' Judith felt obliged to say, 'However, another check-up by Doctor Previne probably wouldn't come amiss – so I'll ring him in the morning.'

She asked the doctor if he would bring the

supply of stronger sleeping tablets he had previously recommended, but when he arrived he confessed to having left them behind.

'I got them ready,' he said, folding his stethoscope after examining Madame's chest, 'then foolishly, instead of placing them in my bag, I put them to one side of my surgery desk.'

'Are they strictly necessary?' enquired their somewhat disgruntled patient. But at least she had submitted to the unexpected check-up, and almost meekly.

'In my opinion, yes,' Judith said, refastening her night-dress and helping her to sit back against the pillows. 'We've almost run out of the others, and you will need something stronger if you are to have a better night than last.'

Doctor Previne stood wiping his spectacles and pondering. 'I cannot manage to get back myself today, I have a conference to attend. But I know my partner has a couple of calls to make in the village this afternoon. If he dropped the tablets at Father Sauvan's place would it be possible for you to pick them up, Mademoiselle?'

'If it's for my benefit Heinzmann can drive her there,' said Madame.

Paul, at Judith's request, was the one who delivered the message to Heinzmann. She asked if he would mind doing it when they met at lunch. 'Anything to help,' he agreed cheerfully. 'I'd take you to the village myself – but it's Fenella's half-day and we're going out.'

Judith gestured towards the window and the greyness above the distant mountains. 'Take your macs with you then.'

Heinzmann looked annoyed at having to get the saloon out two days running. For one thing it was having starting problems. Judith heard the motor cut out twice on the short distance between the garage and the house; and while he waited for her to climb into the back the German had to press down on the accelerator to keep the engine running.

More cautious of him than ever since those startling suppositions had hit her yesterday afternoon, Judith sat in silence – while he, for his part, cursed under his breath at the car and angrily ground the gears.

Preparing to climb out at the Abbé's presbytery, she twisted round and her eye caught Garth's old photograph still lying on the window-shelf where Madame had tossed it. Yesterday, after the visit to the bank, it had lain forgotten by both of them. Deciding she had the right to take it again, Judith slipped it into her anorak pocket.

She forced herself to smile at Heinzmann as she closed the car door behind her and he

gave a curt nod. But as she waited for someone to answer her knock at the presbytery
door, she was astonished to see him do a
three-point turn in the road then speedily
drive away.

'He must have misunderstood the
message he was given, he was supposed to
wait for me,' Judith explained to the Abbé,
as he let her in. 'Now I shall have to
telephone the house and ask them to tell
him to return – or start walking.'

'If you attempt the latter, my child, you
may get drenched.' As she had done to Paul
earlier, the priest directed her attention to
the sky outside. 'But do not worry.' He put
one hand on her shoulder and ushered her
towards the fire in his beamed and book-
littered study. 'I shall ring and arrange for
someone else to collect you.'

She was puzzled. 'But who?'

'Garth. He is visiting one of my parish-
ioner's farms today – to discuss the possible
purchase of a second-hand tractor. He
called in on his way. The doctor came with
Madame's prescribed tablets a few minutes
later – I shall ask my housekeeper to bring
them just before you leave.'

'Thank you. It's good of you to co-operate
with us, Father.'

The lines around his eyes crinkled with
humour. 'In country districts a priest's house
makes a convenient half-way depository. In

winter, if any of the minor roads become impassable, we have some very curious things left for collection – one year we had to keep a pig in the garage for nearly a week.'

Once the arrangements had been made with Garth, the Abbé provided Judith with tea. 'Our friend will be about ten more minutes he tells me, and will be pleased to pick you up on his way back. So you should not be long away from your patient after all. How is Madame, incidentally?'

Sipping her tea, Judith was quiet for a moment. 'She seemed to be recuperating all right. But yesterday she was determined to go into town and now she's suffered a slight set-back.'

'I am sorry to hear that.' The Abbé's voice held sincerity – then a thoughtful concern. 'Perhaps on your drive back with Garth you ought to tell him too? I know that he is planning to impress on Madame the need for this tractor he is viewing today. But if she already out of sorts, as you English say, it may not be the most favourable time?'

'No. Not that they ever agree much,' Judith regretfully remarked.

'I fear Garth is too impatient when it comes to bettering matters on the estate. And if there is any difference of opinion on that score, his temper flares and he forgets himself.'

It was on an impulse a few seconds later

that Judith suddenly took the retrieved photograph from her pocket and held it out. 'Father, do you happen to know this man?'

He studied it calmly. Like so many men of his vocation he was rarely hurried or surprised by the human race. 'I know to whom this belongs,' he said quietly. 'But where did you get it, my child?'

'I found it in the grounds of Villiers.' She was sidestepping the core of the story but had to refrain from telling a deliberate lie. 'I've reason to suppose though that it's Garth's...' He nodded and she added: 'I intended to hand it over to him but Madame Ruddler happened to see it first.'

'Oh?' He raised his eyebrows. 'Did she not recognise the sitter?'

'She didn't seem sure. Besides, her mind was on other matters. Should she have done, Father?' she persisted.

He did not commit himself. 'It is possible they met only once or twice and it was a long time ago. Memory fades.'

'But who was this man?'

'A Monsieur de Courgeny. Before the Second World War he owned Villiers. But owing to poor health and the failure of certain business interests as the war-clouds gathered, he could not manage to keep it up so sold to the Ruddlers.'

'Could he have been the owner Garth once mentioned? – the one interested in ornithology who built the look-out on the mountainside?'

'He was an avid amateur naturalist, *oui* – a civilised and cultured man all round. An aesthetic bachelor.'

'But what was his connection with Garth?'

'The Monsieur was his great uncle...' The priest watched the surprise rushing to darken and widen her expressive eyes. 'Yes... so now you see the reason for Garth's deep concern about the run-down state of the land there. He is bound to it by family ties and the love of the heart.'

So this was why he had come to this isolated place and had stayed in spite of his frustrations with his employer? Judith met the Abbé's gaze. 'Does Madame know who Garth is?'

'No, he has always kept it from her. And I am trusting you to do the same, M'selle...' There was a long, audible sigh. 'Perhaps I have erred in disclosing these facts, but it seems to me that Garth needs a young and reliable friend out in that situation. Someone who comprehends the cause of his fierceness as he sees so many things on the estate allowed to decay – and who can support and sympathise with him – even try a bit of restraint if need be.'

It might already be too late for that, Judith thought – sitting without speaking. The other went on:

'I often regret that I was the one to write and inform him of this job. Knowing of his links with Villiers, I should have realised there might be friction sooner or later.'

She longed to reveal how bad that friction could already be. What paths of trouble and intrigue it was possible Garth might have tried. But she couldn't add to the worries of the older man that much. Besides, there was no proof to offer – just a string of distressing circumstantial evidence which seemed to have grown heavier during the last few minutes.

'I shan't break your confidence, Father,' she promised gently. 'Though I doubt I could have any influence on Garth's behaviour – especially regarding his work.'

'You may be mistaken, my child. He frequently mentions you to me, you know? There is a fondness growing there…'

To hide her conflicting expressions, she bent to put her cup on the nearby table. And when she looked up again it was to say: 'Father, where is the M'sieur de Courgeny now?'

His hands opened in a fluttering, impotent gesture. 'Who but God can tell? He disappeared – somewhere in Paris during the German Occupation.'

'Just vanished?'

'My child, this was war-time. People did in those days – and even now some have never been traced. All Garth knows is that his mother and great uncle were together in Paris for a while and that when his mother stood in danger of being arrested for her work in the French Resistance his great uncle tried to help find her the means of escape...'

The day-long greyness still hadn't brought the expected rain. Huddled beside Garth in the land-rover, feeling cold and the talk she had had with the Abbé lying across her mind like an indigestible stone in the stomach, she shivered.

'I'm sorry there's no heater in this old wreck,' he said, showing that for all his concentration on the road he was aware of her every movement. 'You must be frozen.'

'It doesn't matter; I'm only too glad of the lift.' The exchanged remarks gave the excuse to look at him directly. She was keeping the photograph back, having decided that to return it immediately after the call to the Abbé's might seem somewhat coincidental. Hanging on to it another few days would not matter.

It was curious, she thought, how enlightenment could both reduce and increase distance between people. Garth's emotional involvement with the stark beauty of this place and his resentment of Madame's niggardly approach towards its maintenance were wholly understood. But how could she

feel closer to him – when that under-
standing was also showing her that he had
more reason to use desperate measures
against their employer, not less.

'I caught sight of you while we were in
Lourdes yesterday,' she said, as they passed
between the open gates of the drive.

'Did you?...' She was deliberately testing
his reaction – but his face was hard to read.
'I had intended getting Heinzmann to help
me clear some scrub-land, but as his
services were commandeered I went chasing
up a stock of fertilisers for the farms. Cheap
stuff is more difficult to find.' Sarcasm had
pushed through. 'That's the criterion for
each thing I purchase. It's more economical
in the end to buy the best but there's never
enough cash made available.'

'Our outing yesterday ended at the bank.'
Judith was still watching him carefully.

'Yes, Heinzmann mentioned that this
morning.' The sarcasm deepened a little.
'No wonder you now have reason to think
the excursion upset Madame. Drawing out
money personally again must have been
quite a traumatic experience.'

'I wasn't actually there to witness it,' Judith
pointed out. 'She might have engaged in all
sorts of business...' Like that of paying off a
blackmailer. Or paying them off for a while.
One thing was certain, that would not be the
last demand now. Even Madame herself

must be realising that.

'You say the doctor's trying a stronger sedative on her?' Garth remarked. 'Well, let's hope it's beneficial – for your sake as well as hers. And I suppose in the circumstances you won't approve of my confronting her with the question of this second-hand tractor I've just inspected?'

'I'd rather you left it at present, so as not to risk another argument.'

He pulled up just this side of the front door. 'Wait there – and I'll help you down,' he said. But she was already climbing out as he walked round the land-rover – carefully holding Madame's new tablets in her right hand and trying to manage with the use of her left. Somehow, it threw her off balance; and as her feet touched the gravel she slipped.

Sliding against Garth, she felt his arms shoot out to support her and prevent her from falling. Then they were tightening about her waist, pulling her close to him. And his head was bending over her upturned face.

His lips felt rougher and more demanding than they had before. And, for a second, she could do nothing else but remain passive. Her body was weak – and her limbs seemed to be responding to his will, not hers.

But then: 'Please...' Finding a little strength, she tried to push him away. 'Please

168

let me go, someone might see.'

'Would that be so terrible?'

'Well, I don't think it would be wise.'

His arms fell back. 'But who's there that matters? Your friend Gerard Ruddler's still away.'

Colour hit her cheeks. 'What are you inferring? Gerard Ruddler means nothing to me personally.'

'It didn't seem like that the other day, after our trip to Lourdes,' he said cynically. 'When I mentioned he was going away again you lapsed into a state of melancholia.'

That wasn't connected with Gerard Ruddler ... she was about to retort. But what else could she add? That she had been suffering from shock after almost being run down by Heinzmann?

'I told you he was driving around in a growing state of intoxication... The fool probably didn't even realise what had occurred.' Would that be Garth's reply? 'And why didn't you tell me anyway? Why did you keep it to yourself?'

He would surely harp on that.

In any case, she thought miserably, whatever he said it would make no difference. To trust the words or responses of anyone here at Villiers was no longer possible. She now had just one person she could rely on – herself. So she might as well keep quiet, just as she had that day.

Garth, taking her silence as a vindication of his allegation, was swept by irritability towards her. 'You vacillate, that's the trouble,' he said crossly, after waiting for her to speak. 'One day you're still moping over a man who's jilted you and gone – and the next you're behaving as if Gerard Ruddler's opinion of you is the one thing of importance in your life…'

'Oh, don't be stupid!'

The quarrel was insane, filled with its own momentum, and was bound to end with one of them striding away.

It was Garth. Going back to the other side of the land-rover, he jumped inside. Then, without another glance in her direction, he drove at Paul's breakneck speed – and with Heinzmann's rashness – towards the distant garages.

SEVENTEEN

Afterwards, Judith felt shaken. The memory of Garth's arms about her in the past, the nearness of his body and the touch of his mouth brought on a stormy yearning and, as she pictured the scene of this – his second angry departure from her, an obsessive regret.

Until that painful and unexpected end of her engagement, she had moved through the time of her relationship with John in a calm, even smug, way. Why was this so different? She had, after all, cared very much for John. The reason for the failure of that romance could still perplex her. Had it turned out to be too quiet and settled, their future too predictable? Perhaps, lacking the piquancy of the unexpected, it had even become dull – at least to John. And love, needing the occasional spark of excitement to make the senses tingle, had lost its luminescence for them both.

But how did such an hypothesis relate to the muddled state she was in now? Especially to the chaos of her present suspicions. And since she had been told just how deeply Garth was linked to this estate she almost shrank from learning more of the truth.

She wasn't so much afraid for herself now – as afraid for him. If only they could talk, thrash things out.

The notion of rectifying their present estrangement brought her round to the prospect of taking a stroll through the grounds next morning and devising some excuse to run into him.

But her hazy scheming came to nothing. For next day she felt unable to stray so far from her patient's side. It wasn't that she could perceive any definite change in Madame's physical condition. Her radial pulse was still regular and moderately strong. And there had never been the slightest indication that the expert surgery she had undergone in London had had anything but the most beneficial results.

But something was building up. There was a growing inner tension and a glazed look about the eyes. As if the mind beneath had been dragged away to concentrate on one special problem.

The house, too, felt strange. Even with the disrespectful Paul and Fenella in it Villiers had not yielded any of its heavy atmosphere. But now there seemed an added element – a strained, pregnant air of waiting.

'I have heard from Rosa that our other help, Madame Drouet, is coming back,' Marcelle Guis stopped to say to Judith in the corridor that evening, 'so I have told that cousin of yours that she soon must go.'

Was that what Fenella and Paul had been whispering about earlier? Judith wondered, having seen them together in a corner of the hall. She decided to ask them.

Fenella didn't seem depressed by the news of her coming departure, for when she appeared in the dining-room at dinner to add extra slices of chicken to the usual cold fare she was whistling to herself.

'Paul's eating with his sister tonight, at her

172

request,' she said. 'But somebody else is joining you – someone who's just arrived.'

'Who?' Judith asked in surprise – and forgetting her own planned interrogation.

Fenella grinned. 'Your attentive crony, Gerard Ruddler...'

'Madame will be amazed and delighted to see you,' Judith was saying to Gerard a few minutes later. 'I'm sure she had no idea you were coming back so soon?'

'No – and I hadn't the opportunity to stop and let her know in advance. As it was my journey was difficult enough. However, I made up my mind to come back and check for myself on Madame shortly after we finished our call. You sounded so concerned about her, Judith?'

'Well, I was rather,' she admitted.

'Then I am only too glad I have returned to discharge some of my obligations. And that is why I wanted a quick discussion with you before I go on up to the bedroom.' He sat in his usual place after pulling Judith's chair out ready for her, and regarded her gravely. 'I take it that you arranged the doctor's visit as you said?'

'Yes. He came the following morning and popped in again today.'

'What was his opinion? I suppose he did not approve of that sudden outing? Did he have any advice to offer or further treatment?'

'He recommended a couple of day's rest in bed and a more effective sedative.' Turning to the sideboard, Judith filled two plates with salad and chicken. Gerard took his absent-mindedly, still concentrating on Madame.

'Then she is not sleeping well?'

'She slept better last night, though at one point she appeared to have a nightmarish dream. She tossed about and kept murmuring – and I sat with her until she settled down.'

'She spoke aloud?' He had paused, fork half-way to his mouth. 'Did she say anything intelligible?'

'I caught a couple or so words. But by themselves they didn't make much sense.'

'What words?' He leant across the table towards her. 'I ask in case they might provide some clue as to any inner worry she might have.'

'Well, there was a mention of money,' Judith admitted cautiously.

'Ah ... then it may as I suggested to you on the telephone – my sister-in-law is often agitated by matters of finance, needlessly, of course. She should never have gone to that bank so soon.'

His words struck Judith as ironic. But Madame had no choice, she could have told him, a blackmailer does not care to wait... And the memory of her patient that day, taut, the pale face sharp against the window of the returning taxi, came into her mind like a photograph.

Gerard Ruddler dabbed at his mouth with his table-napkin and gave a prolonged sigh. 'What a pity my sister-in-law's convalescence is turning out to be so eventful, Judith...'

Madame manifested quiet pleasure at his return rather than open delight; she seemed too tired to do otherwise.

'Gerard, remember your offer to shoulder the business affairs of the house for me?' she said at one point. 'I may take you up on that at some future date...' and to Judith she said: 'Do you think you could bring my pills and drink early tonight, Nurse? My head's beginning to ache again.'

'Judith?...' Gerard Ruddler followed her into the corridor and called her back. 'I would be glad to assist you tonight or any other night by sitting with Madame.'

'But I couldn't allow you to do that.' Judith was adamant. 'After all, that is what I am paid for.'

She didn't intend her refusal to be a rebuff, but to her surprise he seemed to take it as such. 'It isn't that I'm not grateful,' she added hastily to make amends, seeing his expression. 'And if I do require help, naturally you'll be the first I'll call upon.'

He hesitated, not wholly mollified, but apparently deciding not to fight the issue for the present. 'Very well, my dear. Suit yourself – though I hope you will have a change of mind.'

The nights were turning colder but the expected rain still did not come. It was as if it were bunched up inside the clouds, waiting for sufficient pressure to burst through. Drawing back the curtains of Madame's bedroom early next morning, Judith looked at the barrage-balloon shapes drifting across and dropping shadows onto the ground below. The drive beneath the window turned into a dappled brown and orange.

It was then that she saw Garth. On his way past the house, he was perhaps on the lookout for a sign that Heinzmann was up and about, for his upturned gaze seemed to be seeking out the window of the German's bedroom on the floor above. But the curtains must have been still closed, for he frowned.

Then, as his gaze dropped, he caught sight of Judith and for a second their eyes met and held. If he had given her a friendly acknowledgement she would have immediately waved. But his nod was cool and formal – the kind one might give a passing stranger. Perhaps I should have taken the initiative? Judith thought; but the decision had come too late. His long-legged stride had taken him past.

'What about the doctor?' Madame mused from the bed. 'He's not coming again today, is he?'

'Not unless I telephone.' Judith walked back across the room. 'And I see no reason to at present.'

Not that the past night had been entirely uneventful. For although Madame apparently had no recollection of it, just before midnight she had suddenly passed into that same fit of restlessness. Pushing the blankets off her chest, she had flung her arms about like a windmill; and the muscles of her throat had worked spasmodically.

Bending over her in case she was awake, Judith had whispered in her ear: 'Is there anything *I* can do to help, Madame?'

But the response had been negative. Her patient had remained trapped in the whirling motion of that sudden subconscious disturbance, unable to escape from the tablet-induced sleep. And although there had been a gradual return to a mostly-tranquil repose, Judith – wrapped in the eiderdown from her own bed – had sat in the armchair at her side for a large part of the night.

Marcelle Guis was the first visitor of the morning. As she did most days, she came in to enquire of their employer if there were any special orders. 'Oh, just do as you wish,' was the somewhat weary answer.

'Before lunch, I shall go to the kitchen and consult Madame Guis myself,' Judith remarked later. 'Being so familiar with your likes, she's sure to be able to suggest some dish to tempt your appetite.' Yesterday her patient had toyed with most of her food.

Madame, hanging on to Judith's arm while lowering herself into the chair by the fire, grunted. 'Whatever concoction you rustle up between you, it will hardly be the panacea for my sort of trouble, Nurse.'

Judith regarded her thoughtfully. The formal barrier between them, the boundary separating employer and employee, had never been successfully crossed. Yet in this sour little sally was a note of desperation. And Judith was driven to repeat her offer of last night:

'Can't I do anything to help?...'

'I doubt it, Nurse – I doubt it, very much.' It was no use. The habit of remaining in isolation from her staff was probably too ingrained. And, looking away, Madame deliberately concentrated on tucking her blanket about her knees.

As the day drew on she reminded Judith of a spring being wound to its limit. Under the electric light that evening, the surface of her cheeks seemed tight, as if the underlying nerves were being stretched; and there was a visible vein in her forehead that appeared to be dilating.

The sight bothered Judith, and caused in her a slow but steady growth of worry. Then she began to have the feeling something else was about to happen – the nature of which she couldn't quite define.

Gerard Ruddler had hovered about his sister-in-law's room since morning; and only when Judith began to prepare the invalid for bed that night did he reluctantly retire to his own place. 'But I shall remain alert,' he murmured to Judith on going, 'so if you wish to reconsider my offer do not hesitate to give me a call.'

From nine to ten the minutes dragged. Where everyone else was in the house, Judith could but guess. At last, seeing her patient slept, she took the used cup from the evening drink and returned it to the kitchen. Heinzmann, clutching a bottle, was just lurching through the door, and she had to step out of his way.

'Clumsy oaf,' remarked Fenella, who was standing by the cooker inside and making herself a pot of tea. 'He's just rolled back from seeing Rosa a bit worse for drink, I expect.'

'Every man to his own pleasure,' said Paul, lolling in a chair not far away. He and Fenella still had a conspiratorial air about them. I'm sure they are hatching something up, Judith thought as – having refused Fenella's offer of tea – she went back to her post. She must have that talk with her cousin.

The minutes of the next hour crept on slowly. With the light switched off to avoid disturbing the sleeping woman, the darkness of the bedroom was relieved only by fire-glow. Then, as another few pieces of stoked-up coal were lapped by flames, the colour brightened – and orange flares became red or scarlet.

'Nurse, are you there?' The call from the bed came as a surprise. Hastily, Judith went across.

'Yes, do you want something?...' The time was asked for first – it was after eleven, then a drink. Judith went to pour a glass of water from the jug on the bedside table – but Madame gestured dissent.

'My mouth is so dry – I'd prefer a cordial, please.'

'Very well – I'll fetch you one and add some ice from the refrigerator in the kitchen.'

Pressing herself up from the pillow, Madame flapped a handkerchief before her face – using it like a fan. 'I feel dreadfully hot – perhaps the fire was built up too high earlier on?' But it was never exactly to her liking.

Downstairs the light was still on in the kitchen and the back door had not yet been bolted – which meant that Marcelle Guis had not yet done her late-night round.

Upstairs, there were the sounds of a muted radio, the gurgle of bath water running away, and here and there there were splinters of light from the cracks beneath the bedroom doors. Perhaps in an ordinary household such mundane sights and sounds would have made for a nocturnal homeliness, given the comfortable impression of a family leisurely preparing for bed. But the atmosphere of Villiers seemed to defeat such cosy images – so that one was aware, not of a group of people dwelling charitably side by side, but of an ill-assorted collection of individuals forced together by circumstances rather than choice.

Walking back up the stairs with the cordial and ice cubes, Judith heard the whine of a rising wind. It rose against the east wall and swept to the roof. It sounded eerie, like the ascending wail of a siren, the commencement of some sharp, man-made warning.

The cry that followed a second or two later was, in contrast, even higher-pitched in scale. And the unmistakable clatter of breaking glass that had immediately preceded the cry had already sent one stab of alarm through Judith's senses. It was coming from Madame Ruddler's room...

Abruptly, Judith was racing, taking the last few stairs at a stride and dashing down the corridor towards the partly-open door. She flung it back on its hinges, the cordial in her hands slopping everywhere.

'Madame!' Her patient was lying half-in and half-out of the bed.

It looked soaked and pieces of broken glass were scattered over the top sheet and blankets. The side-table had been knocked askew. But what formed the nucleus of the picture was Madame Ruddler's right arm – very white, flung out to the side with the sleeve of her nightdress slipping back. And blood from a large, open gash on the wrist reddening the carpet beneath it.

EIGHTEEN

There were other cuts about the fingers, but smaller. Judith, trying to staunch the bleeding and having managed to push Madame back against the pillows, gave them a cursory inspection. They could wait though, this gash on the wrist was the most serious, the one that needed attention.

'I shall have to contact the doctor,' she said.

Madame Ruddler's eyes were expressionless. She was pale and shaken. 'My thirst wouldn't wait, Nurse. I tried to pour a glass of water from the jug just to be going on with.'

'I understand.' Judith prevented her from continuing. It was only too clear what had happened. She must have been sitting awkwardly in the bed, attempting to hold jug and glass in either hand in front of her. But the jug had been too heavy, it had slipped and crashed on the tumbler, scattering jagged pieces of glass everywhere.

Leaving another pad of gauze bandaged roughly in position, Judith made to hurry back to the door. 'I'm going to telephone, Madame; but I'll be as quick as I can...'

Still finishing speaking, she stepped out into the darkened corridor – only to collide with the figure that loomed suddenly out of its gloom like a hurtled pebble against a wall. The breath knocked out of her, she stared up – into Garth's surprised face. 'You!'

He held her steady. 'Sorry to have startled you. But there's a gale brewing and I've just been up to Heinzmann to make sure he'll be out a good deal earlier tomorrow morning to help me check for damage.' He broke off, as his eyes focused more directly. 'What's wrong? You look white.'

'It's Madame.' Still panting, she put one hand on her throat as if to force the words to come faster. 'She's had an accident. We need Doctor Previne; I'm going down to get his number and ring him.'

He didn't wait to hear more, he was

wheeling round.

'I'll go...'

'The doctor's number is on the telephone pad on the study desk,' she called after him. 'I put it there in case of an emergency...' Except she hadn't envisaged one exactly like this.

'Any specific message for him?...' Garth then flung back at her. Already half-way down the stairs, he was almost having to shout.

And her voice, as strong as his now, followed his course then echoed round the rest of the landing and house: 'Tell him Madame's dropped a glass and has a badly lacerated wrist. I think she may have cut a vein. And she'll need sutures...'

Who amongst the others heard her first she was never to know. But, abruptly, the corridors about her were erupting into life. And, with startled expressions – and shooting questions at her and one another, they appeared: Gerard, in a velvet smoking-jacket and gripping a half-smoked cigar; Fenella, pulling on a short cotton house-coat; Marcelle Guis, more resplendent, in a dressing-gown of blue silk; Paul, caught in the middle of undressing, and just in his jeans. Heinzmann, too, had heard the row and was coming down.

They were converging on the sick room like any mixture of people drawn towards

184

the dramatic: Marcelle Guis, sweeping forward in almost officious rush, Fenella and Paul – curious but hanging back a bit – perhaps, like a lot of lay-people, a little squeamish but at the same time determined to see something.

'What shall we do to help, Judith?' As she gained the bedroom door and turned to face them, it was Gerard Ruddler who was the first to reach her.

She shook her head. 'I'd just like Madame to be left as she is – as quiet as possible.'

'But surely *I* can do something for her?' Marcelle Guis had stepped forward to stand beside Gerard. 'What about a drink?'

'No. In case the wound has to be stitched under a general anaesthetic there must be no food nor fluids.' Conscious of the ill-feeling her refusal might arouse, Judith was quick to placate. 'However, I daresay the rest of the household would appreciate a cup of tea...'

Doctor Previne, his comfortable old jacket giving some indication of how quickly he had dressed to come out, eventually made his assessment without preamble. 'I wish Madame to be hospitalised, M'selle. Apart from treatment for shock – for that old heart trouble of hers must always be considered – the laceration will need careful suturing in an operation theatre; especially as there may be the possibility a nerve has been affected.'

Having signalled Judith to move away from the bed and follow him to the hearth he kept his voice low.

Their patient, flopping amongst her pillows like a beached and exhausted whale, watched them for a second then reclosed her eyes.

'She seems so introspective,' Judith said reflectively. As if, even in this time of physical pain, the problems of her mind were uppermost.

'Do not forget the effect of shock, M'selle Seton. And, of course, the pain-killer injection I have just administered,' answered the Doctor, misunderstanding. 'There may be secondary shock later, too. I shall have to instruct the nuns at the hospital to be on the alert for signs.'

'Shall I be allowed to remain and nurse her there as well?' Judith asked. 'I should like to.'

'Then I shall enquire. And now, while you explain to Madame what is to happen, I shall go and make the call to the Mother Superior.'

To be private, he went downstairs to use the telephone in the study. Meanwhile, Judith gathered together Madame's toilet requisites, towels and a clean nightdress. Then, bending over the bed, she placed one hand on her patient's uninjured arm and gently roused her.

Speaking of the doctor's plan, she saw the vapid eyelids ease themselves back with apparent effort. '...So I've packed a case for you, Madame. And it's big enough to hold your jewel-case as well, if you wish?'

There was a weak, almost disinterested nod; the injection, combining with the sleeping pills given earlier, was sweeping her down. But then, struggling to express it, she changed her mind: 'No – I'd rather my brother-in-law took care of my jewels.'

'But the nursing sisters are certain to have a safe for patients' valuables.'

'Yes, but I'd prefer Gerard.' Her eyes were closing again. 'Take the key from my neck, please and give it to him before we go.'

It was while Judith was about to put the packed case out ready in the corridor that the woman in the bed spoke once more. Putting the case down, Judith went back. 'Have you thought of something else, Madame?'

But the light from the lamp at the side showed that her eyes were still tightly shut. The large bosom slowly rose and fell.

'It was too much money this time...' Judith was about to return to the case by the door when the murmur made her pause again. 'In the interval since spring they've become greedier...'

Judith bent down quickly. For three nights now this kind of disturbance had occurred and usually about the same time – so that by itself didn't surprise her. But what did was that, unlike the other occasions, the words were so distinct.

'Are you talking about the blackmailer, Madame?' She had a sudden hope of encouraging the other to go on.

There was a long escape of breath. Judith felt a coldness touching the nape of her neck. Madame's eyes were still closed. But there was a tenseness appearing in her face that seemed to indicate she was by no means fully sedated yet. Perhaps her mind was wandering; yet in some strange way it was moving not *from* reality but towards it – clutching for some fragments of truth.

'They know so much – whoever they are. Dates, names of others who must have been implicated in the deals, fees paid – or received. Authentic ... so authentic; things that must be true. Facts that even I had no idea of.'

'Yes, you've said most of this before, Madame – but can't you still make a guess as to this person's, this blackmailer's identity?' Judith's voice was urgent. 'Did anyone here, for instance, ever have an opportunity to learn anything of your husband's past life?'

'*Here?*' It was obvious that the partly sedated mind could not comprehend at once that sort of suggestion.

'Yes, here.' Determined to reach that

undrugged part of her, Judith carefully emphasised each word. 'Someone here at Villiers... It could be someone around you, couldn't it? Almost every person here rouses *my* suspicions... Oh, if only you would give me permission to go to the police, Madame.'

But the effort was being wasted. The other woman's mind was again withdrawing. And, kneeling down beside the bed, Judith saw her face relax.

The room was quiet. Nor was there any sound from the rest of the house. Or was there?... It came no louder than the sighing respirations of the woman in the bed; yet it seemed to run beneath that sound like a sympathetic reverberation. Like mingling with like – the noise, or so Judith suddenly imagined, of another person breathing; someone standing outside in the corridor. Listening.

If she had considered her next move longer she would not have been so clumsy. But, immediately straightening, she brushed against the bedside table – making the lamp base rattle. Consequently, she was hardly surprised on reaching the corridor to find that the snooper – whoever it was – had taken the warning and gone.

When Doctor Previne returned he had Fenella in tow. 'I bumped into this young lady in the hall. I thought she could assist us in dressing Madame in extra clothes for the journey. She will need to be kept warm – after consultation with the sisters at the hospital I have decided to take our patient in my car, it will be quicker than arranging and waiting for an ambulance.'

As the three of them heaved Madame Ruddler into her fur coat, Judith said to Fenella: 'The men will be required for the trip downstairs. Do you know where they are?'

'There's nobody left in the kitchen. I was the only one to take up your typically British suggestion about the tea and I made it myself. I presume the others sloped off to get something stronger – and Paul went to dress again. Anyhow, I'll give everyone a shout. It will certainly be a case of "all hands to the deck" here,' she added irreverently.

Everybody, not only Paul, was fully dressed when they reappeared in the doorway. Marcelle Guis was back in her smart navy dress, though her blonde hair was not quite so sleek as usual. Gerard Ruddler, too, lacked something of his normal immaculacy. There was no folded handkerchief in his top jacket pocket and his bow tie was crooked. Garth was the last to arrive. He had Heinzmann with him.

'Considering the weight of our patient,' Doctor Previne told them blandly, 'it would seem only good sense to move her downstairs now – before the injection I have given her acts further.'

Heinzmann and Garth did most of the work – though even the massive German was perspiring freely as they reached the doctor's car. Madame was put in the back, wrapped in blankets and supported by pillows.

'I shall fetch the saloon and follow you,' Garth told Judith, as he helped her to clamber in beside her patient afterwards. 'Then I'll be able to drive you and the M'sieur back from the hospital whenever you wish.'

She hadn't noticed until then that Gerard, after going back upstairs to fetch his sister-in-law's case, had come down and settled himself at the side of the doctor in the front of the car. 'Very well – thank you – although I'm hoping I'll be allowed to remain with Madame.'

It was a hope to be blocked however. The nuns at the hospital, though treating her with the utmost charm, turned down her suggestion. As M'selle did not speak fluent French and some of the Sisters had no English, one explained, it might make for confusion. Besides, it was not the custom of their particular order to permit outsiders to do their work.

The Doctor's rueful smile told Judith she must acquiesce. 'Why not take the chance of having a break, M'selle? And you must not worry, your charge is in good hands.'

Standing there in the white tiled corridor, she wished she could have said to him: 'It isn't only her accident that concerns me, Doctor... Our patient now lives under the threat of continuous blackmail – she has confirmed that to me tonight. And I am beginning to be afraid of what this black-mailer might try to do to her next, now she is practically helpless.'

NINETEEN

Dawn was approaching when Judith, having eventually returned to Villiers with Garth and Gerard together, wearily climbed into bed. Drawing back the curtains, she lay and watched it.

But there was nothing very romantic about this particular dawn. The coming light was sickly, and the dark surround appeared to be resisting its advance, so that after a while it began to resemble a struggle – the night against the day, white against black, one force fighting off another. Then, although Garth's expected gale did not appear, it rained hard for over an hour.

The room became colder and Judith

shivered. Her body felt chilled and her mind was heavy. To be parted from her patient, knowing what she did was a cause of harrowing anxiety to her – although reason tried to press on her that Madame Ruddler could not be in a safer place for the present, and that, surely, not even the most avaricious of blackmailers could strike again quite so soon?

On Gerard's behalf, she rang the hospital several times that first morning and after-noon. 'They will keep you better informed than any layman like myself,' he remarked.

He hovered around her throughout the day, as if being able to draw on her profes-sional know-how was vaguely reassuring. And in the early evening, driven there by Garth, they both went back to the hospital to make their first visit.

They didn't stay long. Madame, still ashen-faced and wrist heavily bandaged, seemed too sleepy to cope with visitors.

'She'll probably feel more sociable tomor-row,' Garth commented afterwards. He had looked in once – then gone to wait in the car.

Gerard nodded. '*Oui* – the nuns suggest we come about the same time.'

'I suppose the cut hand is all right?' Garth turned and glanced directly at Judith – who was sitting in the back – for the answer.

'Thank goodness, yes,' she said. 'It was

sutured under a local anaesthetic, they told me. And Doctor Previne's come to the conclusion it should heal without complications. He still wants her kept under observation in the hospital, though, for at least a week.'

It was Garth who helped her out of the car at Villiers and afterwards she deliberately lingered until Gerard Ruddler had walked into the house ahead of her.

'I want to give you this, Garth...' Having slipped back into the driver's seat, he was grappling with the big saloon in the same way as Heinzmann – once the engine had been allowed to die it was difficult to restart it. Twice on the journey back the motor had spluttered and almost stopped.

'What is it?...' He glanced round and surprise hit his deep-set eyes as he saw what she was pulling out of her shoulder bag – his photograph. 'How do you know that's mine?'

Momentarily, she considered lying – but then, feeling sure Father Sauvan would forgive her, she told him the truth. 'I happened to see you drop it near the garage one day – and I'm aware of who the sitter is,' she confessed. 'I was curious and showed it to the Abbé.'

He gave her a long, intense look – then an ironic half-smile touched one corner of his mouth. 'You know what they say about

194

curiosity?...' he said quietly.

'Yes. I'm sorry – perhaps I did wrong, I shouldn't have pried?' There was so much she wanted to add. If only he would help her. But it came to her suddenly that – when all she had wanted to do was to close the gap caused by that silly quarrel, to talk in a natural way again, to touch on personal things – her admission, even the photograph itself, might have pushed him further away than before. Her impetuosity in handing over the photograph right in the open like this might be to him the height of indiscretion – and leave him wondering what other *faux pas* she was about to commit. After all, it was obvious it was a matter he had wanted kept private – yet she had already blurted it out in an almost public place.

Desperately wishing she had been more restrained, she rushed to another subject – not caring what it was – before he could speak again: 'Well, I suppose I'd better go in – though I can't think how I shall pass the time these next few days with Madame away. The nuns remain adamant about not allowing me to stay with her.'

'Why worry?' She found his gaze still uncomfortably thoughtful. 'Read a book, put your feet up – or take your favourite walk up to the bridge... There's no-one in the house with the right to raise any objection.'

195

But he was underrating Marcelle Guis. Taking it for granted that as usual in the absence of Villiers' mistress she herself would assume complete charge of the staff, she quickly made it clear that now Judith's nursing duties were temporarily suspended she considered her to be under her orders.

'Try to keep out of her way like I do,' was Fenella's advice, when Judith found she was expected to help with the clearing away after lunch.

Judith grimaced. 'That's easier said than done.' Using her own initiative, she had spent the morning preparing her patient's bedroom for her eventual return; she had changed the chair covers, repaired a cushion, polished the furniture. But even then Marcelle had not left her alone. Popping in and out at such frequent intervals, she had purposely made Judith feel she wasn't to be trusted in the bedroom by herself not, amongst their employer's belongings.

Still smarting under those unspoken insinuations, Judith made up her mind all at one. 'As soon as we finish this I'm going to take my off-duty,' she told her cousin. 'We're not going to the hospital again till tonight – so, as the weather's brightened a bit, I might as well go for a stroll.'

At least it would get her out of the house and give her the chance to think. That seemed to be all she could do for the

196

moment – think. Talking wasn't possible. Not to anyone here at Villiers. Not any more. Even Fenella, because of her ever-developing relationship with Paul, seemed to have a question-mark about her.

Certainly, she must never again voice any of her suspicions about the identity of Madame's blackmailer whilst she was in the house. It was too dangerous. And the remembrance of that unknown person listening outside Madame's door on the night of the accident kept on sending an unpleasant little shiver through her senses.

Absorbed with such reflections on her walk, she was hardly aware of passing the outbuildings or of even skirting the wood until – rounding a corner – she caught sight of Heinzmann swinging what looked to be an axe and striding off into the trees.

Relieved to be spared a confrontation and averse even to be being in the same area, she automatically quickened her steps. The ground was soft after that early morning rain and in places very muddy. She meant to turn back long before reaching the footbridge. But there was a kaleidoscope of colour moving across the face of the rocks above in a way she hadn't seen before – and, suddenly alive to beauty rather than to worry, she pressed forward.

Both feet were already on the bridge when she heard the first crack. It was soft, just audible. The second was louder, making her halt. The ominous sound of splintering wood came again – and again...

The bridge was going! A cry in Judith's throat struggled for freedom. Then died. Jump back, jump back, her mind screeched.

But her legs wouldn't move. She seemed to be paralysed. Then, to her horror, she had a sensation of falling...

But no, it was only a product of her terror. In reality her legs *had* obeyed her brains. Just as her hands had – and the rest of her body. Leaping backwards, striving to make the safe ground, she clutched desperately at the thin spiky branches of an over-hanging shrub. And she had a swift, sharp picture of pieces of shattered wood – before the bridge collapsed, creaking and groaning, into the gully below.

Face drained of colour, nausea filling her mouth, she struggled to get up from her knees. But the pain shooting through her foot pricked like knives and she sank back.

Keep calm ... you could have been killed. The dry little admonition might have been coming from somebody else. Sit down – examine the damage...

The foot was already swelling and any movement hurt; but at least she could turn her ankle. There might be torn ligaments, a sprain – but she was almost certain there wasn't any fracture.

She was still trembling and feeling sick. But how was she to get back to the house? No-one would come looking for her. Probably nobody would even miss her till after dark.

She would have to try and make it on her own.

TWENTY

It took her an age to cover even the first part of the track. Hobbling, sometimes hopping – and leaning heavily on a stick which she wrenched from a tree – she passed by the wood again.

For the first time since coming to Villiers she would have actually welcomed seeing Heinzmann, but there was no sign of him. I shall be lucky if I reach the garages, she thought, gritting her teeth at another stab of pain.

But, pulling herself together, she struggled on. Then, at last, the roofs of the outbuildings came into view – the tops of the walls then, as she rounded the next bend, their whole length. Letting the stick bear her weight, she stood on one leg and rested the injured ankle again. It had swelled more during the journey and the flesh strained against her loosely-fitting casual shoe.

When she reached the outbuildings, she promised herself, she would take the shoe off. Bracing her shoulders, she began to hobble on once more. She took another couple of steps – and then, to her utter relief, she saw a figure move out from the right. It was Garth.

She started to wave and call. He must have happened to glance in her direction even as she began. For she saw him stop abruptly – and stare at her as if he couldn't believe his own eyes. She changed to a frantic beckoning and called out louder.

But now he had started to run. 'You're hurt!...' As he came nearer he was indicating her raised foot and firing questions:

'What happened?... Did you fall?'

'Yes.' The relief at knowing she had help and at feeling his arms supporting her then gathering her up made her go limp.

'It was the bridge, one of the boards gave way... I'm lucky not to have been more badly injured or even killed. I can't think what made it go – it looked all right.'

He stopped her from continuing. 'I'll check that later. The important thing is to get you back to the house.'

With long, quick strides, he carried her down the track towards the garage. The land-rover was parked in front and he hurried her across to it.

'I'll drive you the rest of the way. We'll go right up to the front door – and as soon as we reach there I'll ring for the doctor...'

She didn't want Doctor Previne called out to Villiers again. But Garth, backed by a vociferous Fenella, was insistent.

'Better to be safe than sorry,' Fenella stated, helping Judith to lie on the bed while Garth went downstairs again to telephone.

'Isn't that so, M'sieur?' she threw at Gerard Ruddler – who had come to stand in the doorway.

Rather pale, dabbing delicately at a bead of perspiration on his upper lip with his handkerchief, he hesitated. Then, looking directly at Judith herself, he murmured his agreement.

'It is best Judith. Forgive me, but I do not care to see you suffering...'

'I could be much worse,' she said, forcing a smile at him. 'But I'm afraid the Doctor will conclude that we English are extraordinarily accident-prone.'

In the event, however, it was Doctor Previne's partner who came. And he quickly endorsed Judith's own tentative diagnosis – she had suffered a severe sprain. 'You need time and rest, M'selle. Old-fashioned remedies, yes – but still the best. As for the pain, I shall prescribe tablets and cold compresses and some liniment.'

Before Judith went to sleep that night

Garth dropped in to check on her yet again. 'Have you everything you need?' Somehow he looked slightly gauche in the middle of a feminine bedroom; and, self-consciously, Judith tugged the drooping shoulders of her nightdress back into place. 'Thank you, but Fenella's been extremely attentive.'

Fenella's zealous care would have probably amazed her own mother – though, as Fenella was candid enough to admit herself, the constant trips to the sickroom also presented a way of escape from the more mundane chores down in the kitchen – and from Marcelle Guis' critical gaze.

Surprisingly, Marcelle had been in to see Judith several times. But they hadn't been the most congenial of visits. And Judith had been initially mystified as to why Marcelle had bothered – unless it was to refer to the extra work her incapacity was meaning for Villiers' staff.

'I shan't be here long I hope,' Judith had defended herself.

'But bad sprains sometimes take weeks to mend.' There had been a significant pause. 'Would you not be better at home?'

'Home!' The idea hadn't occurred to Judith and her mouth had dropped in astonishment. 'Do you mean return to England?'

'Yes, you could take your time getting back on your feet then. There would be no rush. It could be arranged...' The manu-

202

factured persuasion had been syrupy. 'I am sure M'sieur Ruddler would be extremely sympathetic. We would get Heinzmann to drive you to the nearest airport and put you on a plane to Paris – then on to London. We might even arrange for a car to be waiting for you there.'

You would go to that much trouble to be rid of me?... Judith's unvoiced question had lain in her eyes. But why? Was it because Marcelle was becoming jealous of Gerard Ruddler's frequent calls to her room?

It was true that he was being even more attentive than Fenella. But that was probably because – like Paul – he had no specific work in the house to keep him otherwise occupied.

Even on her final visit that day Marcelle did not give up. 'You have thought again of my suggestion?'

'I want to see my case through to the end,' Judith doggedly told her. 'I can't think of deserting Madame at this stage – even if I do have to nurse her with a limp.'

Marcelle's clear-skinned face rapidly hardened. 'Very well. But you may change your mind...' What was that meant to be? some sort of threat? 'After all' – it was Marcelle's last arrow – 'you may come to the conclusion that for a nurse who is not a hundred per cent fit herself to take her full salary is not right...'

'But who would look after Madame when she comes back?'

'I would – naturally. I have done it before and could do so again.' She had said that, backed by Gerard Ruddler, shortly after her arrival – Judith remembered. Marcelle had never wanted her here.

But at least her brother's attitude was different. In fact Paul was inclined to cheer her up by pretending to view the accident as a bit of a joke. 'I bet you did it on purpose,' he teased, 'just to force our friend, Massingham, to carry you about in his arms like that. It was a ruse, *non*, for the sake of love – *pour l'amour?* And now you lie there looking glamorous – and keep on raising the poor chap's blood pressure.'

Judith smiled – but thought how ironic his comments were. 'L'amour' hadn't prospered at all by this affair. For even in the midst of Garth's apparently genuine concern for her there seemed a certain stiffness – especially after he had come across Gerard Ruddler sitting intimately beside her bed.

Whether the gap between them was to be permanent or temporary was a question to be answered only by time, she thought sadly.

It was twenty-four hours after her mishap when Fenella – bringing up an afternoon cup of tea – broke her own news. 'I've just had my marching orders,' she announced.

'Marcelle Guis says that as Madame Drouet is coming back next Monday, I've to leave this week-end.'

'But that's so soon.' A shadow was falling across Judith's face. 'And where will you go?'

Fenella flopped down on the bed. 'You know what Marcelle proposed? – that I go home and take you with me.'

So she was still on that tack? 'What did you say?'

'That I was certain you wanted to stay on here.' Fenella's grin was impish. 'Well, I knew you wouldn't care to leave Garth... Marcelle wasn't very pleased. In fact she turned furious when Paul came along at that point and told her about our plans.'

'Are you two off together somewhere?'

'Yes – to Paris for a while.' So that's what their secretive chatter had been about? 'Then, when his ski-instructor's job begins,' Fenella continued, 'I'll join him in Austria.'

No wonder Marcelle had been angry. She might be eager to be rid of the irksome English for various reasons – but she wouldn't want Paul to depart just yet.

'Especially with me,' said Fenella – frank to the last. 'She tried to dissuade him – even indulged in a spot of blackmail ... said she'd help with the future instalments on his car, but only if he stayed. He turned her down.'

Which was one big point in his favour,

205

Judith conceded. At least it proved he must have grown very fond of Fenella. She hoped they would fare all right together. Perhaps they would have a stabilising effect on each other? Gerard Ruddler had once remarked that when the right girl came along Paul would start to settle down.

But as for her own reaction to Fenella's leaving: life was strange; a short while ago her cousin's imminent departure would have come as a relief. Her arrival and presence in the house had definitely been something of an embarrassment, and the deception practised on Madame Ruddler as a consequence had never failed to sting Judith's conscience. But, lying in the darkness that night and imaging Villiers without her cousin, Judith actually feared the coming isolation. And it made it hard to go to sleep.

Dozing fitfully, she suddenly awoke about midnight. Outside, the wind was blowing into the gale that Garth had anticipated much earlier. And inside there seemed to be the sound of lowered voices and steps in the corridor.

About an hour after that she was roused again – though at first she couldn't decide by what? There had been a sound outside but she couldn't define it – except that it somehow reminded her of the breathing she had heard outside Madame's room on the night of the accident. But surely someone wasn't standing on the other side of *her* door now?

Lying very still, she listened – but couldn't be sure. The minutes dragged on. Then suddenly, on an impulse, she struggled out of bed, stumbled across the room and, twisting the key in the door, locked herself in.

She had never done that before – not even after the stolen ring had been planted in her room. And there was something markedly meaningful about the act. For it denoted in her a sudden – and complete – loss of nerve.

TWENTY-ONE

Judith, her leg throbbing, hardly slept throughout the rest of that night. And at six a.m., before anyone else was about, she unlocked the bedroom door and shuffled painfully down the corridor to the bathroom.

Rosa was the one to bring her breakfast. She was late and looked disgruntled. 'I expected Fenella,' Judith said.

'She is arguing with Madame Guis about something,' Rosa answered darkly. 'I think she wants the day off. That means I shall have to get the breakfast on my own today and there is an extra one.'

A short time after she had stumped off, Fenella herself appeared. 'What's this about Rosa having an extra breakfast to prepare?' Judith remarked, after replying to the queries about her ankle. 'Is there someone else in the house?'

'Yes, Garth. He moved in late last night apparently. Marcelle had to make up a bed for him – which couldn't have pleased her.'

So that accounted for the voices and steps in the corridor?

'The wind blew the chimney down off his old cottage and sent it crashing through the ceiling,' Fenella continued.

'He wasn't hurt?' Judith quickly interrupted.

'No, he survived intact. I daresay he'll be in to see you later. At the moment he's across there assessing the damage.' As she spoke, Fenella made herself comfortable on the end of the bed. It was then that Judith realised she looked much smarter than usual.

'Are you off to town? Rosa mentioned you were fighting to get a day off.'

'I'm having to return to San Sebastian. Remember the belongings I had to leave at the hotel there? Well, now I'm heading for pastures new I'm popping back to collect them. Paul was supposed to be driving me – but he's woken up with a headache. So he's loaning me his car.'

'But are you covered by the right

documents, international driving licence and so on?'

'Oh, that's all taken care of,' Fenella said airily.

'You'll be sure to be back by this evening?' Judith asked abruptly, as her cousin rose to leave. Somehow the prospect of being here at night, shut in on her own and greatly incapacitated – and without Fenella somewhere about the house – suddenly seemed very frightening. Last night had been bad enough. And, in spite of Fenella's cheerful reassurances, she felt strangely apprehensive.

Her cousin had been gone about half-an-hour when Garth came in. Smoothing back his wind-blown hair, he apologised for his mud-spattered gumboots. 'I've been checking on that bridge,' he told her. 'But there's nothing much left. One can only suppose that the wet earth had allowed the bottom of the end supports to slip out of place – and your weight did the rest... I did once warn you to be careful after rain.'

As for what the weather had done to his own cottage, he said: 'I doubt I'll be able to go back there, not until full repairs are done.'

'I noticed how precarious that chimney pot was on the day I arrived here,' Judith remarked. 'Surely Madame won't object if you arrange to have that job carried out immediately?'

'I shall ask Gerard Ruddler to raise the subject when he visits her. Though I understand she's still rather drowsy. He's planning to go in early this afternoon – so Heinzmann will take him.'

Judith's own afternoon passed extremely slowly. Tired, she tried to have a nap but couldn't. The happenings of all her days at Villiers whirled around her brain like a flock of noisy starlings. Real birds on the other side of the window pane twittered as it began to rain.

With Fenella away, no-one apparently considered bringing her any tea. And when Rosa, due to go home and already untying her overall, knocked on the door just after five it was to deliver a message.

'The girl – Fenella...' Rosa, in a hurry to get away before the weather worsened further, used few words, 'she is on the telephone.'

'My cousin!' Judith almost exclaimed – then recalled in time that Rosa had never been told their secret.

'I have switched her over to the 'phone in Madame's room.' Rosa had obviously remembered the telling-off she had received from their employer on that score – when she had not put Gerard Ruddler's call through to the extension.

'Judith, is that you?' Fenella sounded relieved. 'Oh, I'm glad *you* were able to come to the phone. I don't particularly want to speak to Paul – I might add to his headache.'

'You've not crashed his car?' Judith said at once.

'No, it's not that bad. But by mistake I left it parked here with all the lights on and the battery's run down. Now, to add to that, the garage has discovered some kind of electrical fault. And they can't get the small part they need till tomorrow morning... So I'm having to take a room for the night.'

'You're staying in San Sebastian? You're not coming back?' That flicker of apprehension Judith had felt earlier was suddenly a vivid spark. She had felt nervous enough last night: anxious, alert, heart jumping at the slightest sound... But how much worse was she going to feel tonight?

'Can't you manage to get here some other way?' she heard herself demanding.

Fenella, with some justification, expressed surprise. 'But, darling, what would be the point? I'd only have to come straight back tomorrow to collect the car. It'd be crazy.'

'Yes, I suppose so. It's just that I've begun to feel so alone here...' Her voice faded.

'Is your ankle bothering you more?' It was the obvious target for Fenella's sympathy.

'No, not really,' Judith said.

'What is it then?'

'Will you wait a moment?...' She limped back across the room and made sure the corridor outside was empty and that the door was tightly shut.

'Well?' Fenella prompted curiously when she picked up the telephone again.

Judith hesitated, keeping one eye on the door. Then, abruptly, she was speaking in an urgent whisper: 'When you get back, will you come with me to the French police about that blackmail business?... I haven't told you this, but it's started up again. And I'm certain the blackmailer's someone in this house.'

'You can't be serious? One of us!' Fenella was having to raise her voice, there was a buzzing on the line. 'But what evidence have you?'

'Only circumstantial, I'm afraid.'

'Well, that won't count for much. And wouldn't it be best for Madame Ruddler to approach the police herself?'

'She won't,' Judith said.

'Then what can you do, darling? And don't forget – if you expect me to back you up – I'm supposed to be leaving at the week-end.'

'That's why we've such little time now,' Judith said desperately.

'Well, we'll talk about it on my return...' It was clear that Fenella had made up her mind to humour her – that all this sudden upheaval must be due to the accident. 'So don't worry – and in the meantime will you find some gentle way of telling Paul what's happened to the car and to me? Give him my love and...' But the line had gone dead.

'Are you still there?' Judith said.

There was no answer. Just a sudden faint click.

Judith was wondering just where Paul was when he knocked at her door and came in. He had looked quite bilious when she's seen him earlier in the day but now, after an afternoon's doze, his colour was normal. Unfortunately, as she began describing Fenella's misfortune his sister walked in to inform them that dinner would probably be late.

Somehow, Marcelle looked amply satisfied to hear about the car. 'Paul should not have been so rash as to lend it,' she observed drily. It was her one comment. Perhaps if she had ranted as expected, Judith would have felt less uneasy.

'At least it doesn't sound like an expensive job,' Judith consoled Paul afterwards. 'Fenella's over-night stay will cost the most.'

'We shall make up the money in some way,' he replied blithely.

She watched him thoughtfully as he left. Once she had seriously suspected *him* when mulling over the theft of the ring. She had known he needed money. He still did for that matter. But so did the others: Marcelle – for her dreamt-of restaurant; Heinzmann; Garth... Inevitably, her thoughts passed on to the blackmail money – and ended in the same old confusion.

Gerard Ruddler and Garth seemed in unusual moods that evening. Gerard appeared reflective; and Garth was edgily pessimistic. 'This wretched wind and rain,' he said, by chance turning up to visit Judith at the same time as the Frenchman again. 'They're creating havoc. Makes one wonder what'll happen tonight?'

Gerard nodded. 'Yes – young Paul Guis has informed me that the telephone line is probably down. He was attempting to call a hotel in San Sebastian. But it is now impossible to ring anywhere.'

So that was the reason why Fenella's call had been cut short? Judith thought. As for Paul, he must have been ringing Fenella's old work-place in a futile bid to locate her and ascertain she was still all right.

Her visitors had no choice but to leave when Marcelle Guis carried in her tray a short time later. 'Your meal is now in the dining-room, gentlemen,' she told them crisply, 'so perhaps you will not linger here too long? I have to do everything myself tonight.'

Lacking appetite, Judith managed a portion of the cold meat then placed the used tray outside her door for easier collection. Afterwards, she hobbled back to bed. Everything that was happening seemed destined to

214

increase her sense of isolation. Fenella was away; and now she couldn't contact a soul outside this house – even by telephone. Tired because of her previous disturbed night, she lay back against the pillows. Then, unable to bear the light shining directly into her eyes she switched it off.

She didn't mean to sleep. And when she woke and found it was after ten o'clock a feeling of disorientation possessed her. Her dreams had been exhausting – and horrible. In one she had been back on the bridge – and falling again... Only this time she had not survived.

Was that what someone had really wanted?... And planned for?

She sat up abruptly, feeling as if she had been struck by a jet of icy water. Why hadn't she considered such a possibility before? She had speculated endlessly on the idea of someone wanting to scare her out of the house, out of her job. But she had never, until now, never thought of anyone wanting to be rid of her so much they would try – even in that clumsy, haphazard fashion on the bridge – to be rid of her for good.

With a shudder she remembered Heinzmann, axe in hand... Could he, working under orders and being paid, have knocked those supporting ends of the bridge out of position? Knowing full well that one day soon she would be sure to walk up there and try to cross. There couldn't be a person here who was ignorant of her frequent treks to the rocks.

But what had happened these past few days to make her quick disposal necessary? To alter the position? Feverishly, she tried to summarise recent events. What of her naive disclosure to Garth that she had discovered who he was ... his tie with Villiers? Could that have been the catalyst? Her unwary naming of a motive for blackmail? If so, his transfer to the house so soon after her 'accident' would be extraordinarily sinister. He might be thought to be moving in upon her, to try and erase the previous failure to silence her.

Then there was her declaration of her suspicions to Madame just before she was taken to hospital – her voiced belief that the blackmailer was right here. It was almost certain that someone had overheard that. And she had repeated the same suspicions to Fenella today – and, no doubt damning herself completely, had talked of at last going to the police. Yet, for once, she had been so careful – had checked the door, the corridor...

It was then she remembered that curious click after Fenella had been cut off. Someone downstairs had been tapping their call! How stupid she had been not to have realised that at once. Fenella had been right to infer she must still be suffering from the shock of the accident.

But who had been in the house at that time? Definitely Marcelle and Paul. Possibly Rosa – who mightn't have gone after all. Heinzmann must have been back from the hospital with Gerard Ruddler. As for Garth – it was unlikely he was still out working with the weather so wet. So they could have all been there. Any one of them with the opportunity to pick up the downstairs' telephone in the study?

The danger she had known in her dreams suddenly fused with the danger she now realised was hers in reality. And she was struggling to her feet. She must lock herself in again; keep everyone out.

Then, tomorrow, as soon as it became light, she would leave. She would go to the Abbé Sauvan, not risk waiting for Fenella, he would give her the advice she needed and tell her what to do. He might even take her to the police himself.

But reaching for the key in the door she froze. It had gone. Alarm tightened every muscle. And the knowledge that someone must have crept into her room and removed the key while she slept was odious. Whoever had taken it intended that her room would be easily accessible. That fact was clear – and so was another – they meant to come back during the night.

I must leave straightaway, was her next overwhelming thought; not stay a minute longer. Tomorrow might be too late.

She dressed at speed, throwing on trousers, sweater and anorak. Then, grimacing with pain, she put on flat shoes. Finally, she slung her bag across her shoulder and stepped into the dark and silent corridor. She slipped down the back stairs as quickly as she could and into the unlit kitchen. The door was still unbolted. Some minutes later, she was limping painfully and all too slowly down the drive, becoming wetter by the second.

A clap of thunder reverberated around the sky above her. But the moonlight was brighter than she had expected, and to escape it she kept to the shadows of the bushes at the side. Now and then she was forced to stop altogether to rest her ankle.

Another, closer, clap of thunder made her jump. It was followed by a streak of lightning that illuminated everything – the dark bulk of the bushes and trees, the surface of the drive – her own position.

The driver of the car coming quietly after her and rounding the bend she had just left must have seen her standing there as if caught in a spotlight. Momentarily, her cry constricting her throat, Judith stood transfixed. Then, as she heard the car door open and the driver climb out, she was trying to run.

She knew it was hopeless, that the figure behind was gaining on her with every step. But she went on. 'Let me go!'

As large hands closed on her arm and she recognised them as Heinzmann's, she struggled and shouted. But she was as powerless as she had been in her dreams; and as he dragged her back to the car there was nothing she could do about it.

She had the impression he was about the shove her into the front – but suddenly someone sitting in the back opened the rear door. Heinzmann pushed her roughly towards it.

Gasping for breath, losing her balance and falling onto the floor of the big saloon, she had no option but to pull herself up onto the seat. Then, as her eyes made the necessary adjustments enabling her to make out the person sitting in the corner and the small glinting revolver half-hidden beneath one hand, she started. 'You!...'

TWENTY-TWO

The person facing her was Gerard Ruddler. 'Yes, it is I... You left your door open – and luckily I happened to notice... Even so, to find Heinzmann and order him to fetch the car and come after you has taken valuable minutes...'

But his cryptic remarks were being pushed aside, Judith was rushing on: 'I should have guessed before that you were the blackmailer!'

'Are you pretending you had not?' His eyes stared at her in the darkness.

'I never – even – considered you,' she gabbled, aware that Heinzmann had gone round the car and was climbing back into the driver's seat. 'I thought – of – others...' It was too painful now to recall she had ever once suspected Garth.

'I do not believe you.' This wasn't the suave Frenchman she had known, but a hard-faced stranger, fighting for himself. The mask was off. And, ironically, it had been Fenella who had pierced its surface. She had never liked Gerard Ruddler.

'In any event,' he was saying, 'You have discovered too much. I always feared you would in your position – that is why I stuck so close to you, why I tried to get you out of the house long before this.'

Where was Heinzmann going to take them? Fear was running over Judith's skin like the rivulets from her rain-soaked hair. As she heard the German having the usual engine trouble and wrestling with the starter, she sent up panic-stricken prayers: Don't let Heinzmann manage it. Flatten the battery. Do anything. Please...

'Unfortunately, my little schemes regarding you – the ring – the bridge – came to nothing,' Gerard Ruddler was continuing. And he spoke with sudden self-disgust. 'They were ill-conceived, too chancy – and I made silly mistakes. Anyhow, you seemed to possess an ability to foil me. Until now... I know, though, that there had to be a last attempt to stop your progress as soon as you mentioned the police to your cousin this afternoon on the 'phone.'

Even through her growing panic, Judith felt a lurching surprise.

'Yes,' he said. 'I have known of your relationship to each other for a while. Marcelle eventually told me.'

Her prayers had not been answered. Heinzmann had finally succeeded; the engine had begun to purr. In contrast Judith's voice was rough with another wave of terror. 'I suppose Marcelle also helped with the carrying out of your various plans?' she shot out bitterly. 'The blackmail and everything else?'

His response contained contempt. 'I would never trust a woman that far. I installed Marcelle in Villiers merely to keep me informed of what went on in my absence and, since my sister-in-law refused to let me take over her affairs openly, to help me maintain some control of the house. Though

Marcelle made one mistake – and annoyed me by engaging your cousin just to please her brother.

'Certainly, I have used Marcelle these past days to try and urge *you* to leave – but in that she was my unwitting pawn,' he said with satisfaction. 'She was simply reacting as anticipated to my deliberate attempt to rouse her jealousy.'

A cruel sardonic note struck his voice. 'You should have taken up her suggestion about going of your own accord while you had the chance, Judith...'

The car was rolling slowly forward into the blackness of the night. It took Judith a terrible effort to try and maintain even a veneer of calm. But she had the compulsion to keep the other talking, to divert his attention from the gun in his hand.

'But how could you! How could you blackmail the wife of your own dead brother?'

'Step-brother,' he corrected curtly. 'There was no special bond between us. Besides, it is circumstance that makes one stoop to such ends.'

'But with your style of life you cannot be a poor man.'

His lips twisted. 'Style takes money – and I lost what I inherited from my wife. I had bills...' there was a flashing reminder of all his forwarded-on post '...and gambling debts. And I became involved with people who do not care to wait for payment. That is why I had to go to Monaco – to try and persuade one of my hounding creditors to give me longer. But as he baulked at that I eventually had to blackmail my sister-in-law for more – and send her to the bank again.'

'But when that last letter of demand arrived, you were supposed to have returned to Paris?'

He shrugged. 'I merely went as far as Lourdes and pretended to board the train. I stayed to send the letter and waited till the money was delivered. Unluckily, you over-rode the command to my sister-in-law that she must go to the bank alone ... so you learnt a bit more. That much was obvious when I later questioned you over the tele-phone. So I was forced to return. However, it was just as well since your patient had also begun to babble dangerously in her sleep.'

'No wonder you wanted to get me out of the room and sit with her yourself,' said Judith, remembering. But her throat was drying up like old used sandpaper as she saw they had reached the gates at last. Heinzmann turned the saloon into the dark and empty lane.

Her fear recharged, she fought to continue with what she was saying: 'All the while you were in the house you must have been eavesdropping on me – and plotting how to put more pressure on Madame.'

'I didn't have time to wait for her demise to obtain her money,' he barked cynically. 'You told me yourself the prognosis was fairly good. So I simply made use of information gained ... which I came upon by chance. Being young in the war I never guessed what my stepbrother was up to in Paris with the Nazis – his lucrative dealing in purloined works of art. And I might never have known – had I not stumbled across his secret and extremely indiscreet war diary just after he died. Wanting to assess how much he was worth, and with my sister-in-law in hospital at that point, I had ample opportunity to search the whole house.'

'But why blackmail? Surely Madame would have helped if you had told her of your difficulties – she's fond of you.'

His sarcasm was like a lash. 'Not to the extent of parting with large sums of cash for gambling debts. No, threatening to expose the past activities of her husband was the only fast way of obtaining the amounts I needed.'

'But the events, they happened so long ago ... and her husband is dead. Why did she refuse to go to the police?'

'Because I also threatened to implicate her.' His half-smile came out as a leer. 'She still retains what was made from the spoils of war, doesn't she? Do you think she does not dread having to give that up? She may not have been fully conversant with my step-brother's affairs – but she was never interned and, as an Englishwoman, she must have realised that was odd and that they were coming out of the war unscathed financially. Some of her jewellery can't be accounted for legitimately either – that's why some pieces have never been adequately insured.'

So that's why she had always been so concerned about her jewel-box? Judith thought dazedly. It really had carried secrets – as Garth had once jokingly implied. It also explained why she had deferred to Gerard Ruddler's suggestion about hiring a private detective when it came to the missing ring, she couldn't afford to have the police in her house even for that.

'Any kind of accessory is in an invidious position,' Gerard Ruddler was remarking.

The car slid on. Heinzmann, showing no interest in their unintelligible English, kept his gaze on the road ahead. The wind rose higher and the rain bounced viciously against the toiling windscreen wipers. To combat another wave of total panic, Judith searched wildly for something else to say. Her eyes were huge in her ashen face.

'You talked of Paris – I heard a rumour that the man from whom your step-brother bought Villiers was there, too, during the war…'

She didn't expect any comment – and it came as a shock when Gerard Ruddler said with indifference: 'There was a mention of him in the diary. He came across my step-brother, it seems; turned up begging for help to get a niece into safety. A female Resistance worker, I suppose... It did him no good. My step-brother, remembering him as a cultured old man, feared he might have recognised a stolen painting he had in the flat and engineered his disposal.'

The word sent a ripple of horror into Judith's blood. 'Disposal?'

'Yes – at the hands of the Gestapo.' The information was given without emotion.

Judith's horror turned to sickness – then, as she pictured the aging worried man, to a scorching pity. Unthinkingly, she made to brush away her sudden tears.

'Keep still! Don't move.' The cutting command jerked her up like a puppet. Gerard Ruddler's fingers were taut about the trigger of the revolver. Her already pounding heart beat faster.

'What do you intend to do with me?...' Her voice shook. 'Are you going to pay Herr Heinzmann to arrange another "accident"? So far, you've mentioned the ring and the bridge...' Momentarily, she recalled his almost silent reaction to her safe return that day and his pallor. What she had seen had been a man facing the prospect of another failed plan. 'But you can't have forgotten the incident of the car?'

'The car?' he repeated harshly. 'I know nothing of any such incident.'

'But Heinzmann nearly ran me down in Lourdes – the afternoon I went in on an errand for Madame. Didn't you pay him to get me injured – so I'd be useless to go on nursing her?'

'Your imagination must be fevered,' he rapped. 'I'd have hardly tried such a scheme in a town. If Heinzmann did do that I daresay he was near intoxicated and probably oblivious of such a thing happening. Pedestrians who've barely escaped with their lives from *his* driving must be littered all over the place. Anyhow, apart from handing over the usual tip for the occasional favour, this is the first time *I* have paid him for doing anything. And he is more or less ignorant of what is really going on.'

'He must be aware you are taking me somewhere against my will.'

'Yes – but he believes we came chasing after you because you stole something from your absent employer.'

'Stole! What?'

'Ear-rings from her jewel-box, a necklace, other trinkets...'

'You gave him that lie!'

'It is perfectly credible. Especially as I also told him I believe you took that ring – then became frightened and put it back. Tonight, you have fallen into temptation again... I have brought the evidence with me, ready to plant on you if need be...' He tapped his overcoat pocket. And she had a glimpse of Madame's silver hair brush. Marcelle Guis would no doubt be very happy to confirm that she had always coveted that.

Gerard Ruddler's tense face held a sudden satisfaction. 'You cannot contradict any story I choose to give to Heinzmann – there is the problem of language between you. Besides, he probably would not listen – our hard-drinking friend is too concerned with earning his extra money. I have promised more, too, if everything turns out right. He will not need to pester your countryman, Massingham, for advances from his coming wage packets for weeks.'

So that was what Garth must have been paying him that day near the garage? A 'sub'?... I have misread so many things, she thought hopelessly; fitted together simple coincidences and made an incredible number of wrong conjectures. And now it's too late to make amends.

'It is ironic, is it not?' Gerard Ruddler suddenly remarked. 'Heinzmann thinks I am taking you to the police and handing you over as a thief – when what I am really doing is stopping you from contacting them at all. I cut the telephone line to prevent that... I did not think that with your injury you would be able to make any further move tonight. But I underestimated you.'

'Obviously, you were the one to remove the key to my room while I slept earlier on,' she said – her voice still weak.

'I couldn't afford to have you locking yourself in. I had to be a hundred per cent sure I could get to you when I wanted – as soon as the others were out of the way, in bed.'

'You still haven't said what you intend to do with me,' she whispered. The fear seemed to have exhausted her, her body felt completely limp.

'I haven't decided yet. My first plan was to force you to leave the country tonight – anything to get you out of my hair.'

'Go tonight?... But I've insufficient money.'

'I'd provide that. And you have wages due that I could commandeer.'

'But what if I – refuse?...' Somehow, even in her trembling state, she managed one last pathetic show of nerve. 'And there's my cousin – she now knows I'd already suspected someone in the house. I could easily contact her later.'

'You are pointing out complications that have long occurred to me,' he retorted darkly. 'Even though I am sure my sister-in-law would never dare to back up your story about her being blackmailed and that any accusations regarding me would be dismissed as the ravings of a lunatic – you will continue to be a danger... And to find some way of silencing you permanently seems more and more the only course.'

She shrank from him on the seat. 'You're mad!'

'Not so mad that I wish to risk spending any part of my future entombed in a French gaol because of you.' His stress making him like an over-stretched bow, he jerked the revolver in a menacing gesture. And Judith flinched.

But then, abruptly, the attention of both of them was snatched away. Heinzmann, cursing audibly, was having to pull up. Instinctively, the other two bent forward, peering for the cause – and made out the shape of a fallen tree. Under the car headlights its rain-sodden trunk lay like a huge brown crocodile across the road. 'The wind must have brought it down,' Judith said.

But Ruddler, barking out a command in German to Heinzmann, pushed her back. 'Stay where you are,' he warned her. 'It is not that large, it will not take Heinzmann long to shift it.'

But for all the German's heaving, the tree was not so easily moved. He had one more try then beckoned and yelled.

'He needs my help...' Gerard Ruddler reached for the door. Then Judith saw him hesitate. He wants to lock me in from the outside, she thought – reading his mind, but can see no way of doing it.

'Try anything foolish – and I'll make you regret,' was his final threat.

Judith, her mind in turmoil, watched the two men begin to struggle with the tree together. Oh, Garth, Garth – she thought if only I'd talked to *you*. Told you what I told Fenella... All this mightn't be happening...

But it *was* happening. And she had to try to escape now – or there might never be another chance...

TWENTY-THREE

The rain hit her like an avalanche as she opened the door and crept out. Her impulse was to flee from her captor by running back towards Villiers. But logic quickly beat that down.

No, she had to get off the road and into the wooded slopes below where no car lights could reach her. Gerard Ruddler had made one mistake – he apparently hadn't thought to bring a torch.

Creeping into the shadows by the low mountain wall, she prayed that he and Heinzmann – both panting and absorbed

231

with their exertions – would be kept from glancing in her direction. Somewhere about here was the short cut to the village that Garth had once pointed out. If she could only locate the gap in the wall... But there wasn't enough time. She realised she had to find cover in the undergrowth at once.

Jerking herself over the low grey stones in one clumsy movement and feeling the impact on her injured ankle send a welter of pain through the rest of her leg, she slid into a tangled mass of brambles.

The fall itself was quiet – but brown, withering ferns crackled under her weight. They caught Gerard Ruddler's attention – and he gave a cry of alarm.

He must have raced back to the car to check on her disappearance first, for three or four seconds passed before she heard his voice again. This time, he was obviously standing close to the wall immediately above her.

'You little fool, Judith! I know you are down there somewhere...' His fury made the words into a rain of lethal bullets. 'Come out – or I warn you you'll be sorry.'

He waited. Feeling as if her heart must burst through her chest, Judith stayed quite still. Gerard Ruddler spoke with more force:

'If you don't come up of your own free-will I'll see to it that you never emerge alive from this place. When the police eventually find you they will assume you stumbled, hit your head against a tree... and Heinzmann and I will testify that you made a bid for escape as we were bringing you in for questioning.'

Wasn't that exactly what he wanted? All he was trying to do was to trick her into giving her whereabouts away by answering back. Judith listened, terror-stricken, but remained silent.

It was evident from the sounds still going on in the road behind him that Heinzmann was continuing with his efforts to dislodge the tree. But any moment now he, too, will follow me, Judith thought despairingly; and with both men beating the undergrowth they would inevitably find her.

In spite of her sprained ankle, she had to push on... Trying to shield her face from the tearing brambles and still bent almost double, she began to sidle forward – keeping to the inner line of the wall. Then she heard it – the noise of a car. Had Heinzmann succeeded in moving the tree then?

Instinctively, she raised her head and searched for moving headlights. They were there plain enough, yellow, bright, sweeping across the night, the rain and the trees. But they were coming from the wrong place...

Heinzmann's saloon was still stationary. These lights zooming in along the road were coming from the village. Half-incredulous but immediately struggling to stand upright, Judith braced herself for a second leap over the wall that night...

'Stop! Stop!...' She came out on the road at a point just beyond the fallen tree and ran like an hypnotized hare, yelling and waving, the agonizing pain in her ankle acting like a spur, straight into the arcs of the approaching lights. Lights – not of one oncoming vehicle – but two. The first was the landrover from Villiers. And as it screeched to a stop, its driver clambered out.

'Garth! Oh, Garth...' At the sight of him she halted for a second, drowned in relief, and began to cry. Then she rushed forward.

'Judith!' He raced towards her, catching her in his arms. 'What the devil's been happening!... Why are you out here? And you're bleeding and wet...'

'Oh Garth, I needed you...' She was already trying to spill out her story, a note of near-hysteria pushing through one disjointed phrase after another. 'It was Gerard Ruddler – he's been blackmailing Madame – he thought I knew...

'Ruddler! Blackmailing Madame?' Garth stared at her.

'Yes,' she went babbling on, 'he paid Herr Heinzmann to drive the car tonight ... he forced me to come with him. He was planning – he was planning to...' But she broke down, still attempting to finish: 'He wanted to get rid of me... Garth, I felt so alone in that house...'

'My darling!' He was lifting her up. 'I was a fool to leave you at all. But I had no idea of all this. I thought you were safely asleep – and that in any event Fenella was due back.'

'She's still in San Sebastian. Paul's car broke down.' She stifled more sobs, pushing her head against the rough tweed of his jacket. 'But where've *you* been?'

'Only to the Abbé's – to cancel our regular chess evening because of you.' She was shivering and clinging to him – as if she would never let him go again – and he was speaking swiftly and attempting to calm her. 'The lack of telephones meant I was forced to go myself – I banked on only being away for fifteen or so minutes.'

But now, she was staring over his shoulder – at the three men, one in uniform, coming from the vehicle behind his. 'The police!' she exclaimed in wonder, half-starting up. 'Who has brought the police?'

'I have,' he told her, 'that's why I've been so long. That tree fell and blocked the road just before I reached it on my way back. So I was forced to return to the village and rustle up some help. The local gendarme came, plus a couple of the Abbé's parishioners.'

His supportive hold tightened suddenly – warning her of something more to come. 'The police wanted to contact Gerard

Ruddler anyway,' he said. 'They've a message for him from hospital...'

She jerked her head back, gazing at him with her wide startled eyes. 'The hospital! Has anything happened to Madame?'

'Yes, my dear, I'm afraid so.' He was trying to tell her as gently as he could, his voice pushing against the wind and the rain, and his arms wanting to shield her from all the hurts and terrors of this night. 'It was extremely sudden. It must have been her heart... Madame is dead.'

Some explanations were over. And some had yet to be given.

Sitting beside Garth in the Abbé's presbytery – where she was being given shelter for the night – she felt drained. What was happening back by the fallen tree she could but guess – a surprised and protesting Heinzmann was still being questioned and Gerard Ruddler had, for the present, vanished.

'It's ironic,' she said quietly, secure in Garth's embrace and the study fire making haloes of light about their pensive faces, 'if he hadn't cut the telephone line, Gerard Ruddler would have received that message direct from the hospital and probably none of this would have happened. It's not likely he would have been bothered about me and my suspicions then – not with Madame, the star witness, gone for ever – and knowing most her estate would now be coming his way.'

'As it is,' Garth interjected, 'he may have a charge of attempted murder to answer; certainly, abduction or something like it. And whether in view of this blackmail – which by his actions he's openly admitted – he'll be allowed to profit by his victim's will is a matter for the French courts to ponder.'

Thinking of her proud, irascible employer, Judith felt a mounting compassion. Madame had been so fond of her brother-in-law. But at least death had spared her the pain of learning what his true feelings were about her – and that *he* had been her tormentor.

They sat for a while in silence – then Garth pulled her closer, seeking her mouth. 'Will you forgive me?...' he murmured after their kiss.

'Forgive you?' she said unsteadily – his kiss had been long but wonderfully tender.

'For my foolish conclusions that you and Gerard Ruddler...' His cheek brushed hers. 'I imagined that, having been so desperately hurt by a younger man you might instinctively be reacting ... turning naturally to someone a good deal older. And Ruddler was always around you...'

She placed her fingers gently across his lips, preventing him from continuing. 'Yes – but now you understand why, and that it wasn't because he found me so attractive.'

They smiled into each other's eyes – the rift between them spontaneously and for ever healed.

'I thought I'd lost you...' he whispered. 'So soon after finding you...'

She wound her fingers around his. Shortly – and sadly – she would have to tell him one more thing, what she had learned this night of his great-uncle, how the old man had died. But she was near to him, giving him her love, ready to share his hurt. Ready to share all there was in life.

And feeling him respond to her warmth, she forgot herself, her past unhappiness, her broken engagement, her growing fears at Villiers, the dying hours of terror and she and Garth were as one.

The publishers hope that this book has given you enjoyable reading. Large Print Books are especially designed to be as easy to see and hold as possible. If you wish a complete list of our books please ask at your local library or write directly to:

Dales Large Print Books
Magna House, Long Preston,
Skipton, North Yorkshire.
BD23 4ND

This Large Print Book, for people
who cannot read normal print,
is published under the auspices of

THE ULVERSCROFT FOUNDATION